DR DEMARR

A HUTCHINSON NOVELLA

PAUL THEROUX

·DR. DE MARR·

WITH ILLUSTRATIONS BY

MARSHALL ARISMAN

HUTCHINSON

LONDON   SYDNEY   AUCKLAND   JOHANNESBURG

© Text Paul Theroux 1990

© Illustrations Marshall Arisman 1990

This edition first published in 1990 by Hutchinson

Century Hutchinson Ltd
20 Vauxhall Bridge Road, London SW1V 2SA

Century Hutchinson Australia (Pty) Ltd
20 Alfred Street, Milsons Point, Sydney NSW 2061

Century Hutchinson New Zealand Ltd
PO Box 40–086, Glenfield, Auckland 10, New Zealand

Century Hutchinson South Africa (Pty) Ltd
PO Box 337, Bergvlei, 2012 South Africa

British Library Cataloguing in Publication Data

Theroux, Paul, 1941–
  Doctor DeMarr
  I. Title
  813'.54
  ISBN 0-09-173612-9

Set in Monophoto Photina by
Vision Typesetting, Manchester

Printed and bound in Great Britain by
Butler and Tanner Ltd, Frome, Somerset

DR DEMARR

1

Out of nowhere, and after years of silence, George showed up one July day and put his face against the screen door and said, 'Remember me?'

He was clowning in the way that desperate people sometimes do. He said, 'Deedee?'

Gerald did not want to open the door. How could he have forgotten the man who had destroyed his life? He wanted to say: *I thought you were dead.* He had often hoped so, but his pessimism told him that it could not be true. George was his brother, his twin, or else he would not have let him in.

The spring yanked the screen door shut with a smack, like the lid of a trap, and the brothers were both inside, jostling.

George was nervous, fussing with his hands and breathing hard, trying to be helpful. He followed Gerald into the kitchen and tripped him – almost knocked him over – he was so eager to please. Wherever Gerald turned he came up against his hovering brother. How different they were, and yet it had always been like this! Years ago, walking side by side, they had bumped shoulders, tramped on each other's toes, hit elbows – 'You go first', 'No, you'. They got in the way, one kicking the other's feet, usually George kicking Gerald's, which was why Gerald resented the memory of being slowed and pushed by that little oaf. That was another thing: they were physically small – just over five feet in high school, and they did not grow any more. Gerald blamed his size on George, too. If it had not been for George he would have been a whole man.

Their father, who had no other children, used to introduce them at parties, saying, 'I believe in having two of everything!' and he insisted they sing 'Daisy, Daisy' while he sat there beaming. In those earlier years they wore the same outfit, had the same haircut and shirt. They wore shorts, knee socks and big-toed, Buster Brown shoes. Because of their size and their comic clothes they were always taken to be much younger than they were. Their father's intention was to make them look the same, but Gerald believed the matching clothes only tended to exaggerate their differences. Yet people did not regard them as two boys, rather as one irregular being, a four-legged freak.

Gerald and George DeMarr were identical twins.

The hateful shriek was, 'It's impossible to tell you apart!' That statement set them apart – it made them enemies. But, being twins, they could not be separated. They were a matched pair. From the first, Gerald and George were not allowed any existence away from this mirror image: each one was a reflection, or an instance of human repetition, or a small biological stutter. They were seen as a double image. Gerald thought: *I am a shadow*, and it was an early mournful memory of his that as a twin he had been buried alive.

They seemed unusual, as physical echoes, and so they were goaded to perform.

'Do something together – sing, dance, recite a poem, pledge allegiance to the flag.'

This was 1951. Their clothes were always costumes – just right for skits and party pieces. They sang songs, they tap-danced until their bow ties shook loose, they did alternate stanzas of 'Flanders Field' and 'The Concord Hymn' (*By the rude bridge that arched the flood . . .*). It was all the hackneyed upbringing of twins – the freakishness of it, the puppet show. People called them the Deedees, or the Dancing DeMarrs. It prevented them from maturing, it destroyed their will-power, and coupled with their

2

small size this meant they would always be treated as grotesques or as children.

'Are you sure *you* feel all right?' a person would say to one when the other was ill, as if it was impossible for them to escape each other's illnesses. They were not two individuals: they were aspects of one.

Their names, too, were given interchangeably, as if it hardly mattered. 'You must be George,' people said to Gerald, and delighted in their mistake, because it was caused by the twins' supposed sameness – and in consequence their flaw was that one was superfluous.

They grew up in Winter Hill, a place that was both a town and a neighbourhood of Boston – from the high ground in the centre of it, looking east, they saw the Custom House tower, and to the west were wooded hills. The area itself was a barely respectable ruin of three-decker houses – dry, rust-coloured shingles and sagging porches – on the steep streets at the very edge of a small city.

Mr DeMarr was a salesman in a men's clothing store that still called itself a haberdashery. It was a badly-paid and boring job, and unworthy of him, but his work had become an easy habit. He was given discounts on his clothes. He dressed like a trial lawyer – pin stripes, a Homburg, a cashmere topcoat. As a young man he had worn spats. He was slightly taller than his boys and very proud of his tiny feet. He told jokes; his wisecracks somehow fitted his natty clothes. The jokes revealed his sadness and his sentimentality. He was tearfully fond of his wife and always spoke to her in a shy grateful way – no wisecracks – because she never judged him and said what he feared, that he was a timid show-off, nearly a coward, who had pinned all his own failed hopes on his twin sons.

'Give them hell,' he always said, when he goaded the boys to dance.

They were Catholics, and there was something about their version of Catholicism that took away their ambition and made them morally lazy: they had heaven and the confessional and the consolations of secret rituals. There was a theatrical element in the Holy Mass, too: it formed the twins and gave them a sense of timing and decorum. You had to perform to be a Catholic! They were altar boys, and then Boy Scouts, and later they tap-danced in the church hall: 'for the Glory of God'. They were discouraged from joining any teams, since competitive sports would inevitably have emphasized their differences. A brief spell on the Saint Joe's softball team proved that – they couldn't both be pitchers, and George was the stronger hitter.

They were routinely given identical haircuts and identical clothes. For birthdays and at Christmas they were presented with identical gifts. Aunts and uncles were warned. If there were not two available of a particular thing, they went without – one was unthinkable unless, and this became common, a joint gift was given: they were told to share it equally. That happened, as the years passed, with the rocking horse, the meccano set, the pup tent, and the radio; each gift – *To Gerald and George, best wishes* – provoked a bitter and damaging quarrel.

For their first fifteen years or so they seemed to share a life as undifferentiated sides of the same person, one standing for the other, or else the shadow, or sometimes the ghost of the other – a sort of maddening mimicry that was vivid because their father had deliberately made them overlap. They lived a strange unseparated life, full of the hot secret dreams that are the sweats of frustration. They were in each other's company the whole time; they went to school together, they slept in the same room, they were never alone. It was symmetry of a kind, but it was ornamental, it went no deeper – all that effort purely for the design.

They had hated each other from an early age; but they knew

5

they had no one else. They were like the last two survivors of a race of people, with their own language and habits and customs, constituting an entire culture, the smallest society on earth, a nation of two.

Yet each believed himself to be totally different from the other. The very fact that they were twins made them obsessive about comparisons, and they never looked at each other without narrowing their eyes in scrutiny or, indeed, without discovering yet another crucial distinction. They glanced at each other in the way that people glanced at mirrors, but they never saw reflections, only differences.

Gerald looked at George and saw a shrimp, with tiny moles on his forearms that were more numerous in the summer; George looked at Gerald and saw a small pudgy coward. 'You're pigeon-toed,' George said. 'You're worse – dink-toed.' Gerald had a cowlick, George had a chipped front tooth. 'You've got big lips,' George said. 'Not as big as yours.' They recognized a vague similarity, but this made them monstrous-looking to each other. Each one seemed dark to the other and thought: I have a light complexion.

They knew that most people lived with the satisfaction that they were single and unique; but it was the fate of twins to be always weighed and compared. For the whole of their early life they were unhappily chained together, and it was torture to them, for the few likenesses they saw seemed like nothing more than ugly parody.

Their parents had connived at making them seem the same, but it hadn't worked; it never worked; the differences of twins were always greater than the similarities, yet only twins knew that. Gerald and George believed this. If they had been in the habit of confiding in each other they might have discovered that in this respect – in this one belief – they were identical.

6   When their mother died – they had just turned sixteen – their

father held them tighter, consoling himself with them, treating them as toys, and goading them more fiercely. He demanded that they succeed, so that he would not be seen as a failure, although he did not know what he meant by success.

They were still at school. 'George did ten laps,' a gym teacher said once, challenging Gerald, who had been ready to give up after eight. He forced himself to do two more, and the next day he ached terribly from the effort.

'What do you mean you don't know how to do quadratic equations?' the maths teacher said to George. 'Gerald is a whiz at them!'

They supposed that George was being stubborn. He had to put in hours of extra study, and still he never got the hang of them.

This dreary competition inspired one day an unexpected response.

The scoutmaster, Mr Seagrave, said, very loudly, 'You don't know how to semaphore?' He always shouted when he meant to be sarcastic, believing that sarcasm was not a choice of words but rather a certain degree of loudness. 'But Gerald knows how!'

They were senior scouts and wore identical green uniforms with white leggings.

George put down the flags. In a flat insolent voice he said, 'I'm Gerald.'

Gerald looked up from his wood carving, and then smiled at his knife. How easily Mr Seagrave had been fooled! It was a crucial victory, because it seemed to disprove what they had instinctively felt, about their differences being so obvious. They really weren't taken seriously at all, they weren't known, they didn't matter – no one looked closely enough to see them properly. It was the world's fault, either indifference or contempt. They thought: We are Chinese.

It proved that no one cared about them. There was no subtlety, no nuance. They were a pair – that was all, like bookends or a pair

7

of shoes. Their own father had not bothered to distinguish between them: 'I believe in having two of everything.'

It made them cynical. When they saw how easily they could be mistaken for one another they played upon the confusion. George took Gerald's driving test, and Gerald took George's French final. George appeared in court as Gerald on a charge of reckless driving – it seemed less serious that way. And Gerald worked as George at the Star Market. This last ploy worked so well they decided to share the job, putting in three evenings a week each, bagging groceries and stacking shelves. This was in 1959, the year they graduated from high school.

All this had unexpected results. Their taking turns, made their differences even greater. Gerald, who had never really learned to drive well, seldom used the car. George was incapable of simple algebra, Gerald was ignorant of history, George of French, and Gerald would have failed art except for George's effort. Gerald had flat feet: the imprints on his foot examination were George's; but it was Gerald's good teeth that saved George from the dentist's drill.

Cynical people, who regarded them as freaks, had made them cynical and freakish: the two boys passed themselves off as one nearly perfect specimen while remaining – they knew – deficient themselves in many ways.

George was the more composed of the two – a talker, an easy conversationalist, full of schemes and deceits. He attended all the college interviews and he made a good impression, both as himself and as Gerald. Gerald had become a silent and somewhat fearful person, and the more George acted on his behalf the more his confidence ebbed.

But the college interviews marked the end of the odd team effort, and soon the pretence was dropped and they were returned to themselves. Their father died – that dapper man who hid himself in his expensive clothes; that puppeteer, that sadist. Gerald and George were relieved and hopeful, and they began to recover, as from a long illness. This death had released them. The important witness was gone. They realized now that their parents while living had intimidated them, made them guilty, and robbed them of glory. Now the twins could quietly succeed or fail, and now that they were free, each saw enormous changes in the other.

Once, they had needed each other in distinct ways. Arriving home late in the day, Gerald had greeted his mother or father with, 'Where's George?' or 'Has George called?' – and George had usually done the same. Each had to know where the other was – what he was doing, and with whom and why. And each was uneasy and vaguely anxious until he had the answer. If anyone had asked them they would have said that they felt closer to one another than they did to their parents.

But the twins were alone now and whatever it was that had bound them together – a fear of death was what Gerald felt – anyway, it was gone. Alone now they often felt hateful, and each received hostile vibrations from the other. This hatred hummed like a bad smell. They were free and they were alone, but what good was it if they were still a pair? Gerald understood what was in George's mind, because it was in his own, yet his was more muted and kinder.

He wanted George to leave him; but George wanted him to die – and not just die, but for the earth to crack open beneath him and for him to be swallowed by the murk and vapour in the abyss. George's poisonous emanations, that smell, said *die*. Gerald felt that hideous wish in George's looks – his eyes darkened at him; in the casual violence of his touch – he had a way of nudging Gerald with his horny little knuckles; in his harsh arrogant voice. And Gerald sensed it sometimes at a great distance, the odour that wished him ill.

Using the insurance money they went to college – different ones; Gerald chose Boston University and George chose Harvard.   9

George flunked out in his second year, was immediately drafted into the army and was sent to Vietnam. He was not killed – Gerald would have been informed of that as next-of-kin. It was one of the sorrows of his life that he did not know what had become of George; he brooded on his brother and felt sad and thwarted when he realized that he too wanted his brother dead.

Otherwise how could he live? He earned his degree, a BA in economics, and he worked in the Boston Navy Yard as a statistician. Sometimes he described himself as a Vietnam veteran and spoke about his adventures.

He could even impress many of the older men – some of them veterans of the Second World War – with the stories. The one about the snake he had found in his bed – not on getting into bed, but rather the morning after, when it had wrapped itself in five coils around his ankle. The tale of the lunatic with whom he had shared a pup tent on bivouac – only when the man had talked in his sleep had Gerald realized the grave danger he was in from this mumbling murderer. The tropical fungus he had contracted, on a shirt imported from the Philippines, that had given him six months of misery and the mottled skin of a giraffe. The nightmare journey under fire from the jungle outpost to the garrison at Danang, dragging his wounded buddy. And this was strange, because he had never been to Vietnam and he avoided war movies, and any mention of the war by a genuine veteran frightened and upset him.

In the stories he told that weren't about the war he was a highly-placed comptroller doing budget projections for Northrop Aircraft Corporation in Long Beach, whose crucial work had produced in him a massive nervous breakdown; or he was a graduate of Harvard Law School, a frequent visitor to London, England, where he went to the opera and watched the Trooping of the Colour, and he had once lived there in a flat near the famous Hyde Park – it was Bayswater, actually, for any listener who was familiar with the city – and in that year of sheer luxury he had spent the vast sum he had won in a card game on the cargo plane that had taken him from Saigon to Frankfurt, a C-130, as a matter of fact. There was a '68 Chevy in the belly of the plane and the GIs, Gerald included, had sat in this air-borne car, playing gin rummy at ten bucks a point.

None of it was true (although Gerald often thought, *But it must have happened to someone at some time . . .*). He was not ashamed of his lies. On the contrary he was secretly pleased and strengthened, and he despised his co-workers in the Navy Yard office so heartily for believing his lies that he became incapable of telling the truth. That habit isolated him and kept him apart and alone.

He lived in the house his father had bequeathed him – George had received a sum of money. Surely he was dead? Twice, Gerald had almost got married – the women were plain and seemed a little desperate and eager to please; but it was they who left him.

Gerald went on living in the three-storey house where he had been born and raised. He lived in a slow spare way, almost monkishly. When he thought about George he felt like a shadow and he blamed George for this. Not that George had done anything in particular that displeased him, but George was alive. Whispers in Gerald's mind told him maliciously that they were still being compared, and this convinced him that he was living in a dumb and buried way and that in certain respects he had already started to decompose. Terrible thoughts – but he lived alone and told lies and there was no one he knew who could dispute his morbid thoughts.

Living alone, he frequently felt invisible, or only partly visible – patchy and far off. It was a feeling of being half there. Sometimes it was misery, and just as often it gave him relief; it added satisfaction to the only real pleasure of his life, which was peering into people's windows.

This spying thrilled him especially in the colder months, in the early darkness of winter afternoons, before curtains were drawn or shades pulled. He could look into lighted rooms and see people eating or standing at sinks. They stared, they fingered their buttons, they touched their faces. It made him short of breath to see these private acts taking place; and the sight of a woman in loose houseclothes, alone, combing her hair before a mirror, always held him and slowly throttled him. It gave him a taste for night-time walks, and for trains; for back yards and certain streets. Until they pulled it down, the elevated train from Sullivan Square had allowed him wonderful window views. How he missed the curve where the train screeched and slowed between Thompson Square and North Station: several nearby windows in a grey house were his particular favourites, and he knew the furniture in most of them and most of the people. All rooms fascinated him from the outside. Just the interiors, those secrets, had an obscure eroticism and always an excitement. But he knew it was pathetic.

This looking through windows stimulated Gerald and gave him imagery for the letters he wrote and the phone calls he made. He imagined that the women he sought were in rooms like these, sitting on those brown sofas with their legs crossed, between the kitchen and the bedroom, wearing a slip or a house-coat, and with the bathroom door ajar.

He wrote often and at length to a number of people, women mostly, ones he had known from long ago, and others who answered the personal ads he sometimes ran (varying his description) in the *Boston Globe*. His letters were moody, allusive, extravagant and full of innuendo – he teased, he gave advice, he depicted himself as eagerly interested in pleasing them but just a bit too busy at the moment to oblige. His sincerity was in his humour and his certainty: a man this sexy and humorous was worth waiting for. He strung them along until they became impatient – irritably demanding that he do something – and when he vacillated they stopped writing.

There was always someone else. He was a good letter-writer. He had the time, he had the solitude, he was lonely enough. He could be chatty on paper, talking easily about himself (the snake, the lunatic, the war stories, law school, all the rest of it), asking questions, being a friend; and in this way he elicited confidences. He was trusted. In his letters he was usually a businessman, a vice-president ('We make an unbelievably boring product called money...'). The letters never revealed what his company actually did, though Gerald always hinted broadly that his best customer was Uncle Sam, as he put it. 'Defence contracts,' he sometimes said. He had a strong sense that it was involved in the weapons industry – not conventional arms, but high-tech armaments, fibre optics, laser guns, heat-seeking missiles. 'Military hardware,' he sometimes let drop. 'Components for the Stealth bomber.' He knew these women were impressed.

His letters were long and fluent and goading, and they frequently alluded to sex – nothing personal but always specific, such as a detailed description of a scene from a movie – *Body Heat* was a favourite source, and so were *The Postman Always Rings Twice* and *Don't Look Now*, and movies with alarming or unusual sex-scenes. Gerald saw most movies, he went twice a week or more, depending on when the programmes changed at the cinema complex – ten screens – at the foot of Winter Hill. But often, after a particularly vivid letter, the woman did not write back, and he knew he had gone too far. He hated that. He did not want to outrage them: he wanted them to write back in the same vein.

His phone calls were similar to his letters. He teased, he chatted, he made oblique references to sex. He mentioned his company, his foreign travel, his experiences in Vietnam. He could talk for hours. Most of the women he had never seen. He liked it when they complained of illnesses they had, or aches and pains, for then he would give them detailed advice on how to get well. He recommended home remedies, food cures, exercises, sleep, *13* fresh air – and he imagined them undressing or changing and doing as he had advised. Medical matters gave him a thrill of power and authority. He enjoyed discussing specific areas of a woman's body – the shooting pain in her arm, the lump in her breast, the tightness in her throat. Then he could ask: How tall are you? How much do you weigh? Do you smoke? What sort of work do you do? Do you sleep well? Any recurrent nightmares? What do you like to eat?

The women were the strangers he saw in those rooms – from the train, from the street. He knew he was lonely and pathetic, and he saw this as an addiction. He was addicted to these whisperings and scribblings, and so were they.

And it gave him a hatred for the young. He did not know why. He had feared and despised youngsters his whole life, but now his hatred was corrosive. He saw them shambling around Quincy Market. He enjoyed their ruin. They were most conspicuous in the summer months, squandering their health and shortening their lives on drugs. He overheard things. 'She's living with this incredible guy!' or 'He's absolutely devoted to his kids!' Such remarks enraged him. But there was justice in all things: they would get the early death they deserved; and he who had never really been able to choose – what twin ever did? – would go on living his shadow life, for he had been shovelled under from birth. And where was George?

Now Gerald was forty-six. People said that twins had two lives, but he knew he had hardly one. Sometimes he remembered the skits and songs – they were mingled with religion, too: God was the unblinking audience for whom every Catholic had to perform his heart out. It was much worse than an embarrassment. Gerald saw that its solemn foolery, its clumsiness and its grotesque pathos made it actually tragic. Tragedy was putting on the wrong clothes and clowning and failing to be funny.

2

So the visit that July day, two weeks before Gerald's summer vacation, amazed and frightened him. The face against the screen. 'Remember me?' The big kicking feet. And one other thing.

'Deedee?' the man said. He smiled at the secret name.

Except for that childish word, Gerald would not have recognized him, and even so there seemed something diabolical about the man in the doorway. The strong summer light behind him had darkened his face and caused the man's shadow to fall like a shroud over Gerald. The man seemed calm in his darkness, but what unnerved Gerald was the man's size: he was precisely Gerald's height. Their eyes were level.

Hateful kids, some of them no more than twelve or thirteen – girls of eleven! – were his height. They roused his fury, yet he did not feel threatened by them. But now he had the experience of looking a middle-aged man squarely in the eye, and it terrified him to think that the man was his brother George.

'Where's your wife?'

Gerald hesitated, then took a breath to explain that he had never married.

But the man said, 'My marriage was a failure, too.'

'I'm not a failure!' Gerald said loudly, but the way he said it revealed how frightened he was – it was a hollow protest.

'Don't be afraid,' the man said – more calmly now. 'I need a place to stay, for a while.'

Gerald said, 'Why did you come back?'

'I never left.'

Still, Gerald wondered: Is it George? George was the past, like an old coat and crippling clothes that Gerald had been forced to wear. He had nearly suffocated from the nearness of his hovering brother.

'Please go,' Gerald said.

He opened the screen door but he stood his ground at the threshold, blocking the man's entrance.

'Are you alone?'

The man peered behind Gerald, and Gerald saw a stripe of light on the face – sunken features, dry lips, bright eyes. It was a glimpse of illness.

'Help me.'

The man moved again, gave his face to the light. It was a small pale mask of hunger, and there was despair in the bony shape.

'Please,' he said.

Gerald stared back, wishing he would shut up and go.

They watched each other, broken-backed, in the same pleading way.

'Deedee?'

That name again: Gerald gave in. He stepped away and that was when George began bumping into him and tramping on his feet.

George did a feeble dance step, tripping twice and looking around.

'Dad's chair,' he said.

It was red leather and its arms were darkened with age and it had itself the look of a seated man – a big red man reading. Some buttons were missing, there were nicks in its black legs. The matching footstool was pushed against the wall.

'He used to sit in it, looking so pleased with himself. He must have been. He certainly wasn't pleased with us.'

George sat on it and hitched himself back, and, dwarfed by the chair, he seemed like a small boy being obedient.

'I don't mind that my feet don't touch the ground when I sit down,' George said.

He bum-hopped forward and got to the floor and went to the mantelpiece. He picked up a souvenir plate from Niagara Falls.

'Except when I'm on the hopper,' George said, finishing his thought. 'It's so embarrassing. I've never told anyone.'

Neither had Gerald, and Gerald had a fleeting glimpse of the little secrets that had once bound them, hating, together.

'It's a good thing you can lock the door of a john,' George said, and frowned at the plate. 'They went to Niagara on their honeymoon. What an obscene cliche. "The honeymooner's second disappointment". They always talked about their ride on "The Maid of the Mist". Memories, Deedee!'

Gerald hated George's contemptuous reminiscences. He wanted him to go; but George kept prowling, his eyes darting from object to object.

'That rocker, the so-called Salem rocker,' George said. 'He was off it, wasn't he?' – and hardly paused. 'This cigar box. Typical of him to smoke cheap White Owls, real El Ropos, and have an expensive monogrammed humidor. What is it with people who love monograms? What aristocratic fantasy do they have in their heads?'

Gerald said nothing, because he was proud of his mono-grammed cuff-links, dress shirts, pyjamas, ties, his gold-filled belt buckle. He told George again to go. George smiled, hearing nothing.

'Their clock. Their carpet – it still smells of Mum's cooking and Dad's White Owls. We used to fight over the knife.'

'It's a letter opener. It's from China.'

'Oh, sure,' George said. He had never believed it. 'That lamp. "You're going to ruin your eyes."' The mimicry of the old man   *17* was perfect. 'You did all the reading, Deedee. I was the man of action.'

Then go – but before Gerald could put this thought into words, George was talking again. 'Doilies. You don't see those anymore. More monograms' – a dinner plate. 'He used to say, "Pass the mouseturd." He called raisins "dead flies".' George put the plate down and picked up a silver cup, monogrammed GDM. 'We used to have two of these. We used to have two of everything. Where are the others?'

'Lost.'

Destroyed – burned, broken, chucked away, junked, sold. Gerald wanted to say so, but he knew it would make this little man linger.

George lifted the flap of the piano and – still standing: he was the perfect height, he could stand and play without bending, the way a child bangs on the keys – he began to play. He clawed chords on to the keys. He sang *Peg of My Heart*.

And his face brightened. It had been waxen, but now it thickened with colour. The tempo changed. He sang *Bye Bye Blackbird*.

They used to dance to that, and found the song melancholy and spooky.

'You don't seem to realize that I am very busy,' Gerald said.

But he wasn't busy at all, and George must have known that. How was it possible to keep a secret from your twin?

'The Victrola,' George was saying. He lifted the lid of the phonograph, turned the crank and put on a record – one from the top of the black stack.

Mexicali Rose, sung by Gene Autry. Before it was over, he plucked it off and played Bing Crosby singing *Sweet Leilani*, and interrupted that too, plopping down Handel's *Largo*, played by Fritz Kreisler, which he left on until the end – he was transfixed by
18   it, and so was Gerald.

Then the needle scraped and repeated in the dead-sounding groove, and Gerald said, 'You have to go.'

George simply stared and put on another record.

'Not many people know that's the *Poet and Peasant Overture* by Franz von Suppe,' George said, whistling through the gap in his teeth.

But the gap in my teeth is much smaller, Gerald thought.

'What do you want me to do?'

'Nothing,' George said. 'You don't have to do a thing. All I want is a quiet place to stay. I'm just paying a visit.'

His tone was almost resentful, as if he wanted Gerald to thank him for asking such a small favour. That was typical. Because George wasn't asking more, Gerald was supposed to be grateful. It was brother logic, and also the tyranny of twins. George's attitude had always been: *Be glad that's all I'm asking – my small request is a favour to you!*

'I don't want you in my life,' Gerald said.

'We only have one life.'

'That means two things,' Gerald said. 'And I mean one. This house is my life – I don't want you in it.'

Gerald was afraid and spoke in a stilted speechy way, occasionally stammering. The *Poet and Peasant Overture* had ended. The needle was scraping again in the groove.

'Look at me, Deedee.' It was one of George's comic voices but it only increased Gerald's fear. George stared at him and did a dance step.

Gerald stammered on, weakening under his brother's gaze. 'But I won't refuse to help you. I know you're desperate.'

'I'm not desperate!' George said and lost his balance.

His genuine panic had a calming effect on Gerald.

'If you're not desperate,' Gerald said – slowly, as if teaching him English, so that he would remember the pain – 'then why did you come home?'

As soon as he said it, he was sorry, because there was no

possible reply. George just stood there and sagged a little in silence. He knew that *home* was failure. They both knew that.

Gerald said, 'The top floor's unoccupied. I'll give you a week. But I don't want to be here with you. I'm going away –'

'Did you keep Dad's cottage at the Cape?'

'– and when I come back,' Gerald went on, afraid of George's sudden interest in the property (he had an equal claim), 'I don't want to see you here. Promise me that.'

'I promise,' George said, and when Gerald handed over the key, George caught hold of his brother's hand lightly – just a squeeze, the same temperature, the same pads of flesh on the snagging fingers, and such a close fit that Gerald hurriedly shook his hand loose.

'Where's your car?'

'Took a bus,' George said.

'One week,' Gerald said, 'starting tomorrow.'

So it was final. George's back was to the window, and shadows had gathered on his face again – the small dark mask that had first frightened Gerald.

George said, 'You look terribly worried.'

'Never mind. That shouldn't concern you.'

'It doesn't. I'm glad! When I see other people suffer I actually feel a whole lot better – sort of relieved that it isn't me! It sounds awful, doesn't it? But most people think that. Most people have devilish thoughts that they would never admit to. They don't even know that you have to be half full of evil in order to go on living. Do you still go to church?'

Gerald only watched, and what looked like worry on his face was anger – the hatred brimming in him at the way his brother mirrored his own empty life.

'I don't want to see you again.'

'You won't,' George said. 'I know better than to ask a favour of you.' It was his *Be grateful* tone. 'I know when I'm not wanted.'

But the key was in his hand, so he had it both ways, as usual.   *21*

He had the favour and he also had the malicious satisfaction that Gerald had begrudged it. And just before he turned to go upstairs he did another soft-shoe shuffle and a little lisping flap of his feet. That was George: when he wasn't stepping on Gerald's toes he was dancing lightly in front of him – but each was a form of gloating.

George had got what he had come for. Gerald thought: But what about the sickness in your face?

* * *

Gerald took his vacation then, two weeks early, and left the next day for the Cape.

He went slowly in his Datsun down Winter Hill and struggled through Boston traffic to the South-east Expressway, the speeding, contending cars bumping over the broken highway. How come it was never fixed, it only got worse, the traffic more aggressive, the road more dangerous. At the *Globe* he saw the time and temperature blinking alternately *July 13* and *81°*, and then the familiar landmarks, the wooden clubhouse of the Dorchester Yacht Club, on stilts like an Asiatic dance hall from one of his jungle lies, the gas tanks childishly multicoloured in stripes that mimicked spilled paint (and one was said to be the profile of Ho Chi Minh), the junction ten minutes farther on, where the right road said *Providence – New York* and the left said *Cape Cod*.

Merging left, he studied the landmarks, a familiar sequence: Grossman's lumberyard, the low buildings in the pines, the photographical lab, Exit 13 with its fast food signs, the Howard Johnsons and *All you can eat*, *Rocky Nook* at Exit 7 (seeing it, George had always murmured 'Nooky Rock'), the totem pole at Exit 5, *Plimouth Plantation* at Exit 4, and *Heavy Weekend Traffic – Expect Delays*, and the first sight over the tree-tops of the hump of the Sagamore bridge span, like a hill in steel. There was a freighter swilling the water of the canal as he crossed it. He sped on to the Mid-Cape Highway and took Exit 2. There, papers were blowing in the road and were flattened against the chain-link fence: the dump. Then the Wing School, the motels, the gift shops, the real estate agencies, the tracks, Colonial Market. How long had they been loaning videos? The cottage was at the marshy end of Ploughed Neck Road. The lawn needed cutting, the front door stuck, the inside smelled of damp upholstery – salt, sand, mildewed sheets, and the foody smell of decayed wood.

He looked around at the lamp, the light, the mirror, the sandpails, the ship's wheel, the broken oar, the stencilled crate, the smooth bits of seaglass – treasures from the tidewrack – and he imagined George saying *I remember this* and *We used to have two of these* in his proprietorial and mocking way.

Gerald bought a frozen pizza at Colonial Market, and baked it, and ate it at the window, looking at the blue-leaved trees and grey sky this gloomy day. He sat down and clamped his teeth together when he imagined that someone was staring in at him – an old woman with a crippled and misshapen mutt on a leash. The craziest ones had dogs like that.

Then he locked the door and fretted, mumbling to himself, on the verge of crying. He knew he was hiding. Buried again.

It was his first visit of the year. He had begun to neglect the cottage as he had neglected his life. The place was full of junk, and it was junk that George would covet – the way someone drowning clings to flotsam, saving himself and staying afloat by hugging a hunk of greasy styrofoam cushion. There was just such a cushion at the cottage. He made a sudden pile of it all – the stack of newspapers, the *National Geographics*, the wine bottles, the paint cans, the jelly jars he had washed and saved, and all his odd frugalities – the drawers full of string and screws and rubber bands and reusable envelopes; and the toys, two of each, everything that linked him to George, the snorkels, the flippers, the goggles, the kites, the skates; he junked it all. He crammed it into plastic bags, and whatever would not fit whole he broke and tore, dismembering it.

A black sea-drizzle crackled like hot fat in a frying pan and the roof became slick with leaks. Someone drove a car too fast for these slippery roads, heading towards Ploughed Neck. Once, long ago, George had tumbled out of a dune buggy and run shrieking up the driveway, across the lawn.

I've just got arrested –

But he was laughing.

– for driving illegally on Spring Hill Beach, he said. *In the prohibited area! Near the nesting terns! We were racing!*

Why was he laughing? Gerald was using paint stripper on a chair, and repeating to himself the sour and precise word *glue*, and wearing yellow rubber gloves – feeling that he looked like a housewife doing dishes.

And you'll have to pay a fine!

No – you will, George said. *I showed him your licence.*

It was the same face to anyone but them.

I'm you, Deedee! You did it!

He went to the Town Hall to pick up his dump sticker. But when he asked for it, the clerk – a girl not more than sixteen or seventeen – did not look up. She was talking to an older woman who was leafing through a travel magazine.

'England's real pretty at this time of year. Plus all that atmosphere. Flowers and that. Grass. Bricks and stuff.' That was the older woman, her head bent over the magazine.

The girl said, 'England,' She took a deep breath, thinking hard. 'I'd kill to get there.'

And then she turned. Such violent words from so sweet a mouth – no make-up on the face, no lipstick on the lips. Gerald watched her. He would not have trusted her an inch.

24   'Dump sticker, please,' Gerald said when she turned to him.

'One landfill permit,' she said, correcting him. She did not even notice that on this rainy day he was wearing a genuine Burberry. Never mind that he bought it in Boston. What did she really know about England?

He studied the calendar that lay on the counter. He had left Winter Hill on the thirteenth. George would have to be out by the twentieth, when he returned.

'I'll have to see some identification,' she demanded. How he hated her. 'Your car registration.'

He produced it, and she seemed not so much to read it as to smell it.

She clumsily copied his name into her log book, and he was reminded of how poorly coordinated unintelligent youngsters could be; how she started to write and then looked around and lost her place; how she started again. She had no concentration, her fingers hardly seemed to work. He imagined that someone so young and blundering could have no sexual sense at all – no violence, no tenderness.

She handed over the sticker, she lectured him on which window of his car he should display it, and he left.

He took miserable pleasure in using it, throwing away the bags he had filled – the toys, the goggles, the flippers, the skates; all George's – and he sat at the dump in his car, among the screeching seagulls, watching the bulldozer push the crates and bags into the pits of the quarry-like place. And the man in charge, with his rake. He liked the dump this week. He enjoyed seeing the filthy refuse covered, and there was something about this great noisy burial of things worn out and used up or pointlessly thrown away that he found consoling.

It was the perfect solution to error and waste and embarrassment, to the toys that had belonged to George. They were lifted by the jaws of the bulldozer and crunched and planted deeper. He imagined that George was in the jaws, lying still – the   25 odd small man – and then lifted and swung around by the bulldozer's shovel-mouth and buried under the burst cushions and the rusted Weber grill.

Then Gerald panicked and had to leave the dump, because only then – with the destruction of Gerald's possessions – had he seen that for nearly the whole of his life he had wanted to kill George, and never more so than now. The thought that he wanted his brother dead, that his genuine happiness had come from the suspicion that his brother was in fact dead, probably killed in Vietnam – this morbidity drove him from the dump that day. He did not want to think of himself as someone with such bitterness in his heart.

But he went back there. The dump was a process of life, and it excited his mind. He chucked away bottles and papers and trash bags with more of George's things; he felt he had junked his brother's childhood and taken possession of the house.

And he sat and watched the gulls squawking over the torn-open garbage bags. He saw apple peels, grapefruit rinds, crumpled letters. He had once written hundreds of letters to a woman who accused him of being a wimp and a dreamer. *They're just words*, she said. But words were wonderful. He told her that: *Words are magic*.

The pronouncement enraged her, and she sent his letters back, nearly all of them – there were so many – in the old manila folder in which she had saved them. She said she was glad to be rid of them. 'I care nothing for them,' she said. Before Gerald destroyed them, in a low negligent mood, he put them on his lap and began to read them. He went on reading, with mounting fascination. They were funny! They were interesting! They contained daily happenings, some of which were true. They were full of life, and they were loving too – always asking after her, cheering her up. Her own letters were flat and complaining and monotonous. Her ingratitude proved that she was selfish and demanding. His letters showed him that he was a good man.

It rained most of the week, so it was either the dump or the movies. And the movies hadn't worked. The movie was one of those summer ones, for kids: a family on a farm, 'If we all pitch in we can make it work,' a sadistic neighbour, some dead kittens, the famous 'drowning scene'. When the struggling bag sank Gerald burst into tears and sobbed into his hands.

His hatred for George was making him ill. It did George no harm at all, he knew, but it was poisoning him. This hatred for his brother was like swallowing his own venom.

He gave it an extra day, to be perfectly sure, and then he drove home – embarrassed as he passed the gates of the town dump, where he had wasted those hours.

There was no sign of George at the house. But he had not come in a car the first time – perhaps he didn't have one?

I will take no notice of his absence. I will pretend it never happened. Yet he wanted to be sure, and so he was alert to every sound. As he unpacked his suitcase Gerald heard a mutter in the wall.

He ran to the back stairs. A radio was playing! So George hadn't kept his promise. Gerald noticed a tap dripping as he crossed the kitchen. *Now you've got to leave.* Gerald braced himself for an argument and trembled thinking, *You gave me your word!*

George was in an armchair. Obstinate: he did not look up. Gerald spoke his name. Very pale and plump – George was dozing. 'Listen!' But George was obviously very sick. Gerald raised his hand to touch him, but the dry grey skin repelled him. His flesh was the colour of microwaved meat. So he whispered 'Deedee?' in a kindly way. But George did not respond, and then he knew that George must be dead.

Turning aside to whimper – it was a strange sound, like his soul leaving his mouth – he saw the hypodermic needle, the bottle, the ashtray, the addict's junk, and was that spilled soup in his lap?

27

3

Gerald had never known such a shock. Even the death of his parents and his guilty clinging grief had been nothing compared to this. This was physical in a paralyzing way, but it was slow and unstoppable, more like a rising tide: wave upon wave of emotion heaving within him and numbing him – sadness, surprise, relief, guilt, doubt, anger, joy. One caused another, washed up and broke, spilling useless surf and rattling his soul loose. Afterwards, he felt purer and slightly weak, as after a sickness.

For Gerald, George's death was more like an amputation – one that had been successfully carried out on his own body. It was as if a diseased and disfiguring part of himself had been cut away, like a blackened frost-bitten finger. It was a horror, and yet he could not think about it without feeling a little sentimental. It had been a necessary thing and, as with the death of his father, it had granted him another measure of freedom. There was justice in its cruelty and, like all natural deaths in a family, it had a savage element of sacrifice.

George had brought it upon himself! The sick gloating man who had said how the sight of people suffering secretly pleased him – he had suffered and died. He had come home and killed himself, either accidentally or on purpose – pushed a needle into his arm and puked his guts out. His face still wore the urgent expression of the moments before death: defiance – he had fought back – and the only signs on his face that he had lost were his blue lips and cold eyes. His small cheeks were full, he was canted forward, plump and surprised.

And then Gerald wondered: Who is this man and why did he come here?

He feared that it might be merely a macabre joke being played on him; and what if he were not George, but just a small stiff corpse, propped on the chair to terrify him – not his brother at all? George was capable of a deception like that; it was the sort of thing George would enjoy. *You're next*, the staring eyes seemed to say. It was so easy to scare someone by surprising him, even if it was only to shout *Boo*!

The belongings in the man's pockets were too few to convince Gerald that it was George. It would have been so easy for George to have planted them. The dead man's face was bloodless and unrecognizable: pale unfamiliar flesh. Gerald caught himself pitying this stranger. Or perhaps it was the sort of convulsed and choking drug death George had endured that had changed his face and removed the resemblance.

What if – Gerald was pacing the room downstairs, glancing at Boston through the front windows – what if it really had been George the other day, but that George had put this corpse here and dressed it in his clothes, given it his wallet and handkerchief: killed this man and thereby faked his own death? It was possible. And if that was the case he was depending on Gerald to report him dead, while he counted his money in Mexico or started a new life in California or wherever, and continued to cast his shadow over Gerald.

In the wallet there was some money – just over forty dollars – and standard wallet items, credit cards, social security card, all George's. No driver's licence. There was a razor and shampoo in the bathroom, and last week's *Globes*, a sequence of three – Wednesday to Friday. Today was Monday. Did that mean that the man had been dead for two days, or had things been arranged for it to look that way?

None of this matters, Gerald thought. But one thing does   *29* matter: secrecy. Gerald was certain he would not go to the police. If it was George, why should he dignify his druggy brother's memory with a decent burial? If it was not George then certainly George had planted it, and he would not do George the favour of reporting the death and aiding him in his pretence.

They were the family reasons. There was a practical reason, too. The third floor was empty because it was for rent – so was the second floor, for that matter. There would be no possibility of a tenant if news of the death got into the papers.

Once, when they were children, the DeMarrs had been visited by their uncle Frank, who drove up in a green Cadillac. Frank was a simple soul and very proud of his car – practically new!

'Let's go for a spin,' he suggested.

'You can drop us off at church,' Mr DeMarr said. He felt Frank was a dangerous driver, especially when Frank was trying to hold a conversation. But it was raining hard, and it wasn't far to Saint Joe's.

On the way, Frank said, 'You won't believe this, but I only paid two hundred dollars for this beauty.'

Mr DeMarr sniffed and became thoughtful.

'Stop the car!' he said at last.

It was so loud, Frank pressed the brake and spilled Gerald and George off the back seat and on to the floor. The four DeMarrs got out and walked the rest of the way to church in the rain, and it was not until they were inside that Mr DeMarr spoke. He did so in a frightening way, hissing the sentence into his children's faces.

'Someone died in that car!'

And someone had died in Amato's duplex – years ago, and the place was still empty. 'You'd hardly know someone died in there,' Amato said. The *hardly* still bothered Gerald.

These recollections came to Gerald as he laboured with the body, slipping it into the plastic bag and sealing it, and then dragging it into the garage and cramming it into a barrel. Upside down, and with the knees tucked up, it was just the right size. That brought back a memory: the pair of barrels they'd had in their act, and how they had been rolled onstage to the well-known song, and the twins had tumbled out and danced.

Roll out the barrel
We'll have a barrel of fun!

That memory continued, offering Gerald another glimpse of himself and George – George standing on his shoulders and wearing a long coat that reached to the floor, so that one on top of the other they made a whole man. It had been a life as little men, dedicated to dressing up and performing, and remembering it roused all the old hatred for George.

The next morning he awoke with a determination to get rid of the barrel. If it was George it was just what he deserved; and if it wasn't, why should Gerald worry? And there, lying in bed, still bitter about his hidden life, he hit on the perfect burial.

He was soon driving down the South-east Expressway, keeping well under the speed limit. After Braintree the traffic thinned out.

The road was straighter, flatter, bordered by scrub oak and dwarf pine. It was a road with few landmarks, the sort that made you reach for the radio knob. The lumberyard, the restaurant, the swamp, the river, the marsh, the totem pole, the distant view of the prison farm – but mainly it was the exit numbers and the place names on signs that indicated your progress on the route – Rocky Nook, Norwell, Kingston, Pembroke, Plymouth, Marshfield, Whitehorse Beach; and for anyone who knew the road well, the smells. Gerald was penetrated with the vibrations of the wheels and he lapsed into a driver's reverie.

In a world of straight flat roads and low trees and cloudy skies he had needed fantasy. He knew that this plain familiar landscape made him yearn for foreign places, for mountains and deserts and oceans, settings in which he saw himself as an adventurer. He felt it was better to dream, to expect no more than dreams; he had

31

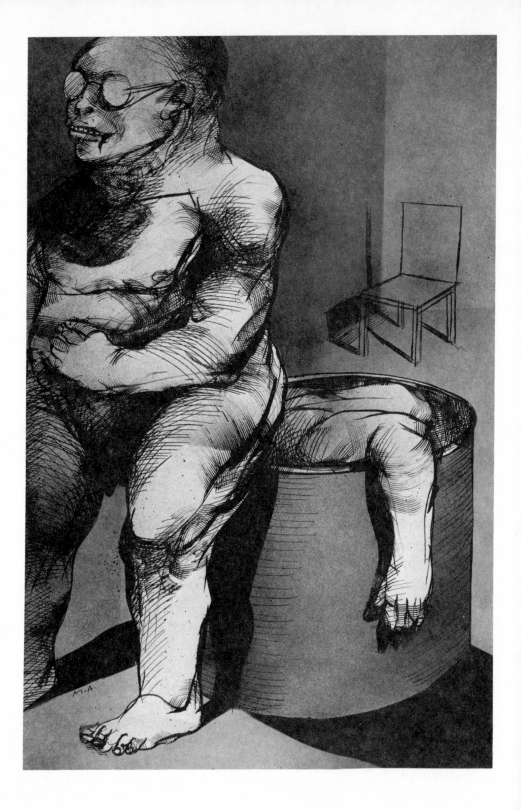

been a success that way. If he had seen real mountains and moors he might never have known such triumphant fantasies.

It was only as he bumped over the steel seams on the Sagamore Bridge that he remembered the load in the trunk; he began watching for the exit. And wondering how George had lived his life.

The dump lay behind a chain-link fence, and today the man in charge was examining dump stickers – making a business of it, halting each car and then, as it came to a stop, hurrying it, motioning with his hands in a peevish way and frowning, as if he found it all intellectually exhausting. Gerald was delighted to find the man there and not guarding the ditch with his rake. Gerald was examined and waved on. He drove down the slope and parked near the narrow trench – it was just the width of the bulldozer that was filling it with the rubbish people heaved out of their cars in sacks and boxes. Among the dust and groans of the bulldozer were the seagulls – large nagging birds that mobbed the edges of the trench, occasionally tumbling in to tear at a burst bag.

Gerald waited for the other dumpers to drive away, and then he slid his barrel out and tipped it against the lip of the trench with the crates of grass clippings, and the smeared cans and broken beach chairs. He rolled it forward and it came to rest just beneath the bulldozed scoop, which covered it with half a ton of sand.

This must happen all the time, he thought. And he imagined the dump to be full of dead men and nameless foetuses and discarded mistakes, and all of it covered with yellow sand and household junk.

He remained – pretending to sweep out his car – until the trench was nearly full and the barrel completely buried. He trusted the incurious dump workers, but he had no such faith in the hungry seagulls. He drove away satisfied with what he had done.

33

'I'm still on vacation,' he said to the empty road ahead. He had the solitary person's habit of holding conversations with himself and always meeting opposition in these dialogues. 'Call this a vacation!'

It seemed incredible that in such a short time he had managed to discover and hide a human corpse. He was a moderate, fastidious and decent man – he felt this strongly. Perhaps this accounted for his efficiency. He had always talked of his adventurous past, and talking had been enough. But now he had acted, he had taken a turning – for the first time in his life – and he had to keep going, to finish what he had started. The burial had made it complete.

He was alone, and so he was solitary in his deceit. It made him feel lonely, but not weak. In fact, he imagined that this secret gave him Power, or at least an authority over his life that he had never known before.

He raced forwards under hot grey clouds that had the shapes of sundaes and luffing sails. The horizon was a row of grinning faces, with monkey cheeks.

As soon as he had crossed the Cape Cod Canal he knew he had succeeded. The canal was like a break in time. He had left the past behind on the far bank: he was safe. There was nothing at all here off-Cape to connect him with the corpse. It was perfect, a buried secret. And anyway, who was there to tell?

He followed Route 3 towards Boston until, at Marshfield – feeling very tired – he pulled into the rest area and parked. The sight of the North River winding through the tall grass below the highway into Norwell heartened him, because it was lovely and unspoiled, and his certainty that it was beautiful gave him hope: If I know that, then I'm still worth something.

He saw that he could leave the whole matter now and go home. No one would ever know. But another mystery, that of George's life, would be his to ponder for the rest of his days.

He sorted the credit cards and rummaged in the wallet as he turned the matter over in his mind, wondering whether to pursue it. That was when he found the laundry ticket – or it might have been for dry cleaning. It gave him a task and a decision. He had a free day and the laundry ticket tempted him. He would follow that lead, and if that did not reveal the life of the dead man he would forget the business and go home.

Printed on the ticket was the name of the laundry and a serial number – no more. There was something important in the little ticket: it had been folded and tucked away. It mattered because it had been forgotten and seemed unintentional. And everything else had appeared so calculated.

He had been so preoccupied with getting rid of the body that he had not considered what his next move should be. But this suggestion could hardly have been easier. It was the Wong Hee Laundry on Stuart Street, the Chinatown exit. If nothing materialized he could just beat it down the expressway to Winter Hill. That was his new guiding thought: See what happens.

It wasn't ghoulish, it was a favour – picking up the dead man's laundry. And Gerald was again reassured by the simplicity of it. It was so easy it could not be wrong.

If he challenges me or asks, Gerald thought, I'll say I'm Charles Leggate – with an 'e' – and my car is double-parked in front of Jacob Wirth's, and I'll have to move it before I can explain how this laundry ticket came into my possession.

And then I'll go underground and never return.

But the elderly Chinese man showed no curiosity and did not even pretend a polite interest in him. He held the ticket close to his face and matched its number to a large parcel in a tall stack. He handed it over and told Gerald the cost: fourteen dollars. That seemed rather expensive for shirts, which was what he guessed was in the parcel. He went to his car and tore off the wrapper and saw that he was in possession of four linen smocks, folded in

35

tissue paper. They were the sort of white smocks worn by so many people these days, not only dentists, doctors and pharmacists, but also art teachers and certain mechanics who carried out car repairs in the more expensive garages.

If it had been shirts he would have headed straight home. But *smocks?*

He could not imagine George the art teacher or George the mechanic. But he clearly imagined a plausible George DeMarr DDM, gouging a root canal, drilling for all he was worth, bearing down hard on a bleeding gum as the patient gagged, his mouth yanked sideways with the hissing drain of a mouth-hook. Behind his white mask George was smirking with satisfaction over the pain he was inflicting.

With this vision of George the dentist, Gerald saw him standing on a stool in order to work at the correct height. But would his vain brother have done that? It was true that dentists were the greediest, the most complaining, the most demanding members of the medical profession, with the highest suicide rate. They simply grubbed for money in people's mouths. That was George's general profile, but George was the wrong height.

He walked back to the laundry and showed the man his ticket.

'I think there was something else in here,' he said. 'Some shirts.'

'No shirts,' the man said.

'Can I see the receipt?'

The man nodded and pulled out a shoebox filled with receipts. After a moment of foraging in the box he clawed out the correct piece of paper.

'Four smock,' he read. 'No starch.' He pushed it sourly at Gerald.

Gerald smiled at the success of his ruse. This was what he wanted to see. D. MARR it said in wobbly capital letters, and there was a telephone number.

D. MARR: was that George's alias or just a Chinese mistake in transcription? The smocks he could see had been hand-tailored. They were not standard issue, but rather custom-made. They were as beautiful as surplices – they could have been priestly garments. Could it be that George had become a priest?

Gerald was the only DeMarr in the Boston telephone directory, and no one named Marr was listed. On a hunch – because of the smocks and because the place was so near – Gerald enquired at Tufts Medical School, just across the street. Doctor Marr? Doctor DeMarr? But no such person existed.

He called the telephone number he had memorized from the receipt. It rang repeatedly – hopeless, he thought: he was calling a dead man's number.

'Doctor DeMarr's office.' It was a woman's voice, and yet not as crisp as it might have been. Perhaps an answering service?

When it sank in – the Chinese laundry clerk had simply written what he had heard – Gerald said, 'Yes, I'd like to speak to the doctor, please.'

'I'm afraid that's impossible,' the woman said. 'He's not available.'

'When do you expect him?'

'I'm not sure. Who's speaking, may I ask? Is this Mr Scarfo?'

Without hesitating, Gerald said, 'No. I'm a consultant immunologist and I'm just up from Plainfield, New Jersey, for the convention here on immunology and,' he took a breath, surprised by his fluency, 'I thought I'd look up my old friend –'

'So it's not an appointment,' the woman said.

'I did want to make an appointment for my wife,' Gerald said. 'It's rather urgent.'

'I was just going to say, we're not taking any new appointments until further notice. Perhaps I can get back to you?'

'It might be easier if I called you some other time. I'm not sure when I'll be back in Boston. Perhaps I'll write a note. Would you *37* mind giving me your address?'

The woman dictated the address: it was a suite on the fifteenth floor of Riverview Towers, Kenmore Square.

The woman repeated, 'Doctor DeMarr is not taking any new appointments –'

'I'll see that all the details are in my note to him. Perhaps you'd be good enough to see that the doctor gets it.'

'It will be on his desk with the rest of his mail.'

Why was this woman being so obstinate and unhelpful?

After he hung up, Gerald parked at the Common Garage and went to Kenmore Square in a taxi. Riverview Towers was not a new building, but it was a stately one, of brick and granite, with ornamented stone around its windows and at its edges, and a heavy stone canopy over its front door that somewhat resembled a movie marquee. Gerald counted the floors to fifteen, and he marvelled at how he had spent his whole life in Winter Hill and had never seen this building or realized that George might still be around. But, thinking about it, he ceased to be surprised; after all, he had always imagined that he had lived a buried life. And now who lay buried?

Still carrying the parcel of smocks – it was like a key to the whole puzzling business – he entered the building and examined the lobby board for names. Among the doctors and dentists, George was listed twice. Gerald gathered that his office was on one floor and his apartment on another. Gerald saw the security guard and thought: I am George's twin – I have a right to be here.

But the security guard did not ask for identification.

'How ya doing, boss?' The guard was black, he looked big and uncomfortable in his chair, the book in his hand was a Bible.

'Warm out there,' Gerald said, with a patronizing smile.

'And it going to get a lot hotter, bo.'

Bo was what the man said. So that was short for *boss?*

Gerald smiled to think that George's security could be so lax – and he was probably paying a fortune for this sloppy protection! The guard smiled back at Gerald, and that emboldened him to take the elevator to the fifteenth floor, and he stepped out and saw the brass plate bearing his brother's name. He resisted ringing the bell. Somehow, he knew it was a waiting room, with a five-foot palm tree, and armchairs, and last month's magazines, and a vast meaningless painting on the wall.

The painting was yellowy-red, the gluey, rubious, ketchuppy paint spread heavily on the canvas like an entire Mexican meal smeared sideways – and Gerald mentally named it *Melting Combination Plate*. It was terrible but it was bright. George had chosen it for its brightness, its colour, probably its size too. Gerald at first hated it and then saw the point of it – and it was better than that waiting-room standby: Norman Rockwell's poster of a freckly big-eared youngster being examined by a kindly old quack with a stethoscope.

He walked up a floor, just to sniff around and see the apartment door, and then he descended to the basement and the parking garage. He prowled on the cool dimly lit floor of cars and saw that the numbered spaces corresponded to the apartment numbers, and that at 1602 there was a Mercedes – lovely, even under its coat of dust. It was a two-seater, light cream with red upholstery, and as with the building and the fresh smell of the corridors and the 'Doctor,' Gerald thought: yes – it all pleased him. And what was oddest was his lack of interest in cars. He drove badly and often said, 'I'm car-blind – car-bored, really' – he couldn't tell one from another. But he knew this one, the 190SL, he wanted it, he was happy here and he was gnawed by temptation.

Everything fitted except the man with the puffy and slightly ruined face who had appeared at the house a week ago and said, 'Deedee'.

Gerald wanted to go home. It was lunchtime. He could sit and fret quietly. I don't know enough, he thought. That worried him. That meant he knew too much.

In the elevator, he told himself that he had punched the wrong button. He got out at fifteen and told himself that he would get the next elevator down. He sniffed and rang the office bell and told himself that he would not go in, even if someone answered. No one answered. He sniffed again.

That was settled then. He called the elevator and waited, wondering what he would do with this parcel of laundry. He had no use for smocks: he would mail them to this address.

The elevator light went on, the warning bell rang, the doors shot apart and a young woman stepped out.

Her stare froze him: she seemed to recognize him, and yet she said nothing. She looked almost fearful, as if she might be wrong. It was an expression he had often seen on a woman's face, though not lately.

This woman had the compact and self-possessed face of a cat, but her skin was sallow and she seemed weary. Gerald saw her eyes flick – she was holding her breath, touching her hair, and in one motion moving her fingertips from her loose blue blouse to her light skirt.

'George.' She made it a sharp word, almost a question, and there was a small sob in the way she spoke it.

She had caught him off-guard, and the words he had been rehearsing seemed feeble and unconvincing: *Just trying to get some information... Looking for my brother... Consultant immunologist... Found these smocks delivered to my office... I called the other day about an appointment... Just visiting... Has anyone disappeared?*

It crossed his mind, just then, that he had killed George and buried him secretly and run off. He was a murderer and his

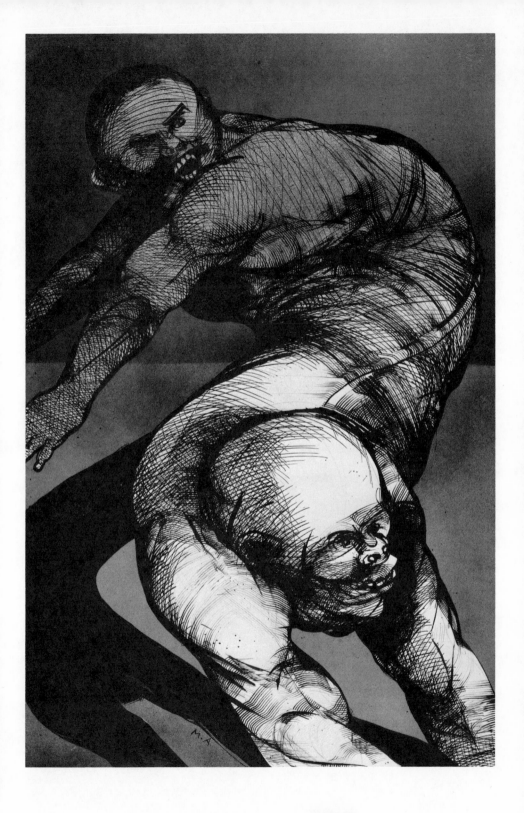

instinct was to conceal what he could and deny everything. The young woman's hesitation, her faltering voice, gave him courage and, fingering the parcel, he began to smile.

'Yes,' he said. 'Are you surprised to see me?'

'No –'

He had made her nervous! But he was annoyed to see that she didn't know the difference. It was that childhood feeling of discouragement when people ignored him by mistaking him for George.

The woman had turned to the door and was fumbling with the lock, trying to be cheery and apologizing for being late back from lunch.

'Don't worry about it,' Gerald said, and stepped inside and thought: He owes me this.

4

He kept on, still sniffing, still sleepwalking, without looking back. He justified himself: I'll get to the bottom of this; then mocked himself with an overtaking thought: It will be over in five minutes.

But he found a reason to feel triumphant. He had not been mistaken for George – no, he had displaced his dead brother. George was dead, and Gerald was no longer a shadow.

The young woman behind him – MISS T. JORDAN had been lettered on her desktop nameplate beneath the five-foot tree, he had been right about that and the bad painting, too – was speaking in a halting way, trying to begin, 'I was getting worried...'

'Glad to be back,' Gerald said briskly, and didn't turn. She *had* looked worried. 'I've had nothing but trouble for the past week,' he went on. 'I was seriously wondering whether I'd make it.'

He knew from a droning ache in his skull that the woman was staring at his head.

'At least I've got these,' he said, and slapped his parcel of freshly starched smocks. 'So I guess I've done the right thing.'

There were other doors at the side of the office – his portion of it. One door led to the examining room, with a high platform-like bed, and a set of scales, and clothes hooks; the room next to it was densely shelved and held bandages and medical supplies – bottles and coils of tubing. Gerald moved swiftly around the office, searching and committing to memory everything he saw –

photographs, books, trays of files, unanswered letters, a diary, an appointment book, and the framed degree displayed on the wall.

He took out a smock and put it over his shirt and trousers. Now he was more comfortable, more convinced of his right to be there: these were the right clothes.

The wording of the degree was in Latin, but any fool could make out that he was a Doctor of Medicine. So George had graduated from Columbia? There were other certificates on display: he was a member of the American Medical Association, he had been voted Man of the Year – two years ago – and here was a framed badge and scroll testifying that George DeMarr had been an Eagle Scout.

Eagle Scout! Gerald knew this was false. Neither boy had earned the necessary merit badges to achieve that rank. Gerald did not mock, but instead was reminded of a shameful occasion at work when someone had mentioned the Scouts, and he had lied, 'I was an Eagle Scout...'

The phone rang. Gerald wondered whether he ought to answer it. Surely the secretary would pick it up? It continued to ring.

'Yes?'

'It's Tallis.'

Tallis?

'You must think I'm crazy,' she said. 'It's just that you took me by surprise out there...'

So Tallis was T. Jordan, the secretary.

Gerald said, 'Come in for a moment, will you?'

She was more relaxed this time – she had composed herself – happy to see him safe, he guessed, and also glad that this stranger was in fact the doctor. He knew she felt apologetic for almost not recognizing him, and he was uneasy, knowing himself to be responsible for her awkwardness.

'I cancelled the morning appointments. There were only three. I hadn't heard from you, I had no idea where you were.'

'You did the right thing.'

'There was another of those urgent calls this morning.'

Another?

'He's going to write you a note,' she said. 'And that Mr Scarfo was here all morning. He wouldn't go away. Mrs Florian is scheduled for this afternoon, and so is Mrs Naishpee – the one with the hyperactive child –'

Gerald was nodding, as though he knew this already; but he was anxious. Who were these incomprehensible patients? And how was he to help them?

'I warned them you might not be in,' Tallis said. 'I could move their appointments. I could cancel. I could do some juggling –'

Gerald was tempted to cancel the whole day – or to agree to it all. He had no idea of the consequences of no, or the conditions of yes. He thought: George was a *doctor.*

Tallis broke off, looking troubled, as she had when she had first seen him outside the elevator. She said, 'I hope you don't mind my asking this, but is there anything wrong?'

Gerald found it easier to face the woman when he saw that she was disturbed. He could not stand a cold stare or a direct question. If she had been blunt he would have felt very small under his smock. But she was tentative, and so instead of feeling like an impostor he could reassure her. He had merely forgotten part of his past. He did not know what sort of doctor he was, or what his mood should be. He had no driver's licence, no keys, no clear image of George the doctor. He knew he seemed vague, but he did not want to stumble so soon. He could not question her. All he knew about this woman was her name. He smiled at her.

He said, 'I'm going to tell you something and I want you to swear to me that you will never divulge it to anyone.'

'You know you can trust me,' she said. 'You have plenty of proof.'

That meant something.

He said, 'And you know you can trust me.'

'I think I do now,' she said. She smiled, and her smile cost her so much effort it seemed to prove the opposite of what she had said – that she had been wounded. 'I mean, now that you've come back.'

He felt that if he was kind he could rely on her.

'A terrible thing happened to me over the weekend,' he said.

Tallis raised her hand involuntarily, as if to protect herself from what he was about to say.

'I had a massive shock,' he went on, gaining confidence.

Tallis had become conscious of her raised hand, and now she covered her mouth with it as she listened.

'Don't be frightened,' Gerald said – Tallis seemed as if she were about to scream. 'I won't tell you what it was. But it's had the most amazing consequences. I feel different, and I have a slight case of amnesia. Certain details, certain objects.'

'I see,' she said blankly. And then, 'Did you say amnesia?'

'Yes, please help me. I don't want anyone to know I've had this unfortunate – this shock. They'll think it's a weakness and try to take advantage of me.'

She smiled again, but without effort now, and without pleasure: it was a memory surfacing in her eyes and mouth. She said, 'You haven't changed.'

What had he done to make her say that?

'Amnesia would be hilarious if it weren't so inconvenient,' Gerald said. 'For example, I can't remember what I did with my keys. I couldn't get into my apartment this morning. Maybe I've lost them.'

'They arrived last Friday,' she said, 'with your driver's licence and your medical ID. They were found somewhere in Boston and an honest person brought them in. I didn't know where you were, or I would have notified you.'

46

She retrieved a bag of objects from her desk, and the keys clanked as she set the bag down on his side table.

She said, 'Don't you believe me?'

He wasn't listening.

She said, 'There are still some honest people left in the world.'

He was thinking: And if I am a doctor, what is my speciality? What do I eat, what do I drink? Am I your lover? But buried in this ignorance was his thrill at not knowing, the risks he was running in being there. That thrill made him incurious and reckless.

He took a step nearer and said, 'Tallis.'

Her features softened and now he believed what she had told him earlier, about being worried when he hadn't come back. She looked so pale. He meant only to touch her hand, but she took his and clasped it.

'I was feeling desperate,' he said.

He had only meant to gain her as an ally, but it seemed to him that she misunderstood. She drew close to him, and then her body rose against his and he could feel her shudder.

Tallis said, 'I know what desperation is.'

So she had misunderstood; but it was a mistake in his favour. He took it as encouragement, he moved his hand to her arm and helped her closer to him. Beneath her sleeves her arms were so thin! Her pallor and her look of starvation gave her a hungry beauty that Gerald found impossible to separate from illness. He felt mingled pity and desire – he wanted both to feed her and devour her.

She said, 'I'm glad you haven't forgotten everything.'

'How could I?' he said.

It worked: she gave him a sorrowful grin and said, 'I was desperate, too – I felt crazy! Forgive me –'

She suddenly broke free of him and stepped away. She had heard something.

47

Gerald was about to caress her – of course, he forgave her! – when she said, 'It's the two o'clock appointment.' She was walking towards the outer office.

'Are you still making appointments?'

'Naturally,' she said. She did not turn. 'I knew you'd be back.'

'I need a little time.' He said he was hungry. Would Tallis go out and buy him a sandwich and coffee? He said he'd talk to Mr Scarfo on the office line.

'Listen' – the voice clouted his ear – 'you're going to help me this time, ain't you?'

Am I – was George an abortionist? Gerald wondered. This man's voice sounded both urgent and threatening. 'I'll do my best.'

'Just do what I want.'

He told Mr Scarfo to come back the next day, but he knew that everything depended on his next phone call. The bogus Eagle Scout scroll and medal had been the first clue; and he suspected the Man of the Year award to be merely window dressing. He decided then to verify the most important document.

'Registrar's Office,' the voice said.

'I'm inquiring about a certain George DeMarr, who apparently graduated from Columbia Medical School in 1972,' Gerald said. He spelled the name and waited until the graduate records were examined. He was transferred to another line; he heard the clack of computer keys and the mutters of another secretary.

'We have no listing under that name.'

He tried the Boston branch of the American Medical Association, and was put on hold. He looked at George's driver's licence and snorted at the mug shot. How could Tallis have been taken in? There was no resemblance at all! But he felt there was justice in this, and it was the fact that he was certain to be exposed as an impostor that made him bold. He would fail, of course – he would wake up from this – and it would be a glorious failure, a wonderful awakening.

But in the meantime he deserved a period of successful stealth. He had spent his whole life meagrely as the dim half of a double image, and it was only today that he had felt any excitement in living. It was like coming back from a sort of underground prison. He did not care about living George's life. I wanted to live my own, he thought – the one I've been denied.

'I'm sorry to keep you. We have no one of that name in this AMA branch. Perhaps it's a new entry –'

This was excellent news, and it excited a responsive feeling in Gerald: with each succeeding falsehood connected with George, the more confidence he had in his own truth. Tallis, in those moments beside him, had helped, too. By returning his affection – he really had wanted to put his mouth on hers.

And he liked the risk – liked it best because it did not matter whether he failed. Even if it all ended now with this patient saying 'What have you done with Doctor DeMarr?' it would be worth it, because he had discovered something that delighted him. George was no doctor – his degree was a forgery. George himself was an impostor!

Gerald ate his sandwich by the window, and then drank his coffee, and carefully brushed his teeth. George was a quack! He dialled Tallis and said, 'Send in the next patient, please.'

She was Mrs Florian, a square-faced woman with beautiful eyes. In her dark dress she seemed heavy, and she moved slowly, staying stiffly upright and using her shoulders in a way that attempted sensuality without quite achieving the effect. It was only when she was seated that her sadness was evident, and then she looked lumpish and stubborn. She brought a strong aroma of syrupy perfume into the room, and there was a pattern on her dress, glittering on the dark silk, of dead birds.

Her file lay before him – the typed particulars and nearly illegible notes.

Mrs Florian said, 'I thought your watchdog wasn't going to let me see you,' and she moved her eyes meaningfully without moving her body.

Gerald smiled in the direction of the outer office, where Tallis sat.

'She said you were busy. That always means something, because busy doesn't mean anything.'

Gerald said, 'I've had a heavy week.'

'I thought she meant you were sick. And then I started wondering who your doctor is. I thought, "Why should I go to him? I should go to *his* doctor!"'

Gerald said, 'I look after myself.'

But Mrs Florian seemed bored as soon as he began to speak. She folded her arms and Gerald guessed that she was referring to her ailment when she said, 'I did what you told me.'

'You did? That's excellent.' He set his face at her benignly to hide the fact that he was totally mystified.

'And it didn't work.'

'What a shame.'

'So you were wrong.'

She was playing a role – using pauses and coyness. That made it especially difficult for him, because he was concentrating hard, hoping for a clue.

Her eyes were deep-set and though they were large they had an oriental cast to them – it was their loveliness – that gave nothing away. Gerald could see pleasure in the pout of her jowls: she was enjoying this.

'And you were so sure of yourself!' she said.

It was a self-satisfied tone – not quite triumphant – and the gloating in it was friendly rather than belittling. It was a sort of bullying intimacy, and it confused Gerald. He wished he had been able to decipher the scribbles in her file.

Mrs Florian said, 'I think it might have made my condition worse.'

Made what condition worse?

'That's extremely...' he began in a ponderous way, and paused, inviting the woman to interrupt.

'I understand how cutting down on smoking might help,' she said, filling the silence he had created for her. 'As you suggested.'

This was a start. Gerald said, 'It was only a suggestion.'

'But don't you see how the anxiety of going without cigarettes might have irritated it more?'

Irritated what more?

Gerald shrugged, and she said, 'Isn't there anything I can take for it?'

'There are many things you can take, but will they do you any good? I'm not sure what the best answer is.'

Because I don't know the question.

Mrs Florian said, 'I've been getting these sharp pains again in the upper abdominal region, and I know it's not peritonitis – we've been through that, haven't we? Sometimes it's agony. Can't you X-ray it?'

'It doesn't always show up on an X-ray.'

'Even with barium?'

He was grateful to her for this. He said, 'Barium's a funny thing. It doesn't always behave itself.'

'Drink lots of milk. That's what my mother would say,' Mrs. Florian said. 'But what did she know about ulcers?'

Ah. Gerald said, 'Some of these folk remedies can be very effective. Milk's not a bad idea. With ulcers you have to be careful in your diet. And alcohol – particularly on an empty stomach –'

Hearing this, Mrs Florian looked hurt. She said, 'I'm obsessive about what I put into my body. I don't eat junk. I don't drink crap. If you want to know, I'm kind of a fanatic.'

She was a big solid woman who, seated, seemed like part of the chair. She was apparently alone and unhappy, and she had the powerful appetite that substituted for a friend in some solitary people. Her loneliness had made her a stuffer. And she was so wounded by Gerald's remark about drinking that he was almost sure she was lying.

He said, 'Obviously, you take care of yourself. That's very important.'

'Worrying about ulcers can give you ulcers!'

'Now this is very true,' Gerald said. He did not know how to go on from this. He smiled at her. She was calmer now. He said, 'Was there anything else?'

She looked amused and resentful, as if he were trying to hurry her.

'Aren't you going to examine me?'

'Ulcers are very hard to examine.'

'There's a sort of swelling,' she said.

'Let's have a look,' Gerald said.

She rose and went to the examining room: she had done this many times; she knew the moves. Gerald heard her sigh as she removed her clothes, and there was something coquettish in the way she sweetened her voice and said, 'Ready'.

She was naked under a short paper smock that she had found somewhere in the room, and she lay on the examining table like a badly wrapped parcel – a body in a small paper sack. Her arms were behind her head and her knees drawn up. Where she was not blackly tanned she was puffy and mutton-coloured, and this unnerved Gerald more than the dead flesh of the corpse he had found in his house and tipped into the dump at Cape Cod.

He fumbled with his stethoscope – listened; fumbled with his watch – felt her wrist; then grunted and touched Mrs. Florian

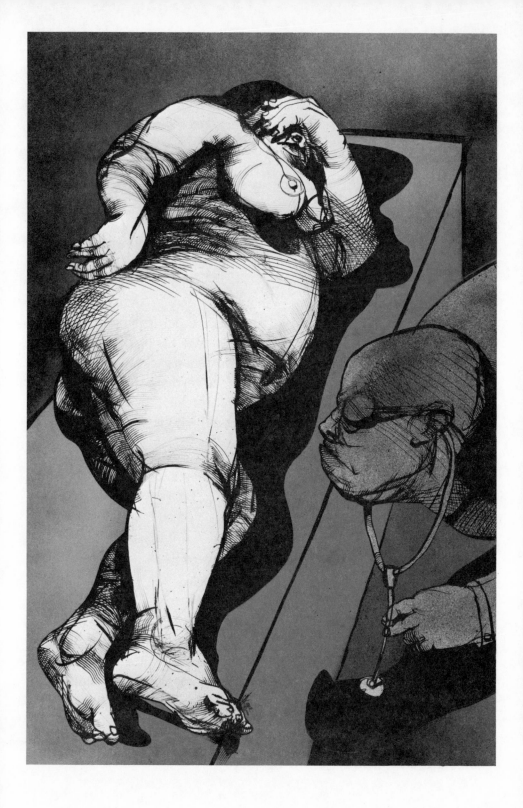

under her breasts, his fingers spread as if playing a chord on her ribs.

'A bit lower.'

He moved his fingertips as she suggested.

'Do you feel anything?'

She said, 'Don't *you?*'

He said gently, 'I see what you mean,' and stepped back, so that she could see him in a reflective mood, pondering her symptoms.

'You can put your clothes on,' he said.

'Aren't you going to palpate me?'

'Of course,' he said, and approached her frowning in order to look serious: he did not want to betray his bafflement. *Palpate?*

She opened her legs and they made a smacking sound as if she was unsticking her thighs. Her face turned aside: he hoped she wasn't smiling. He touched her tentatively, then tried again. He knew now that he could not pretend – he was nervous, and she knew.

'What's the hurry, Doctor?'

He wanted to say: *Don't you see? I'm not the Doctor!*

She said, 'You're always in a hurry.'

Always!

He said, 'I'm sorry.'

'You always say that.'

And then he knew he had succeeded.

The next patient was a woman with a damaged face, Muriel Dietrich. He hoped that she had not come to him about her face. She had not. She wanted him to sign an application that would allow her a licence plate saying that she was handicapped. She said that she could never find a parking place and was sick of walking two miles every time she came into Boston.

'They ask me to describe your handicap,' Gerald said, examining the form.

'Old age – that's the worst handicap of all, God help me,' she said. 'You know what to write.'

He invented a disease and created a Latin name for it, and he defined it in parentheses: 'Progressive wasting'. He was pleased to be able to conspire with this woman against the young traffic cops.

Mr Lombardi – another patient – said he had emphysema. It was an illness Gerald had heard about. He wondered whether Mr Lombardi was telling the truth when he described how he could not breathe and how he slept badly.

He coughed terribly, he said. He used the word 'sputum'. 'I throw up every morning,' he said. He reeked of cigar smoke.

His file showed that George had been treating him for three years for various ailments.

'I'm still taking the medication,' Mr Lombardi said.

He too demanded to be examined.

Gerald took his time and afterwards said, 'Come back and see me after another three thousand miles.' This delighted Mr Lombardi.

'It's my skin tabs,' Mrs Brewster said.

She had come with her husband, an overweight and bosomy man, sixty or so, who had his wife's way of clasping his hands between his knees. He said nothing. When his wife spoke he became nervous and his eyes twitched in flutter-fits of blinking.

Mrs Brewster was asking to be treated with the latest methods. She demanded laser beams.

As she was being examined, she said. 'There's something different about you.'

This made Gerald wary.

'You look happy,' she said.

Ms Frezza made the same comment. She was thirty, she was 'spotting'. It was the Pill, she said.

*　*　*

They were experts on what ailed them. They described their symptoms, they guessed at causes, they suggested remedies. Their physical condition did not match their complaints: they all seemed fairly healthy. Gerald decided that they were reporting progress – they felt a little worse, a little better. Gerald listened carefully and tried to be sympathetic. The rest was ritual – the stethoscope, the tapped lungs, the deep breathing, the pulse-taking, the simple rubber bulb device for checking blood pressure.

Gerald saw that they were not looking for advice. They were suspiciously full of information. They were looking for agreement. Most of all they were in the mood for more medication, and three of them demanded prescriptions.

Between Lombardi and Brewster there had been a phone call.

'You were recommended,' the voice said. It was a tentative request, but when Gerald encouraged him he stated it. 'Thought you might be able to write me a prescription. I'll pay the going rate – I know you're not cheap. The thing is, I've got to have it right away –'

They were not really sick, Gerald thought, sitting with Mrs Naishpee and her ten-year-old son, diagnosed as hyperactive. She was a heavy woman with a drugged and drawling voice that Gerald found maddening.

'How are you?'

'I'm good.'

Her child was practically a monkey, but it was not hard to explain how he had gotten that way. Mrs Naishpee, too, wanted more medication.

Prescriptions were the one item he could not provide – later, perhaps, as he told the man on the phone (who angrily swore at him and hung up). He could not write them, he had no knowledge of drugs, he could not even find George's prescription pad.

But that was his only problem, and it was a small one. He had begun in the confidence that George had been a phoney. Seeing patients was slow work – they were so talkative! But Gerald's nervousness had kept him going and made him attentive. He watched the patients closely, alert to everything they said. They were uninterested in him. They had the selfish concentration of people who believe themselves to be unwell. They were ordinary people whose imagined illnesses had made them superstitious and turned them into egotists. By the end of the day's appointments Gerald was sure that everyone was a hypochondriac. It seemed hugely appropriate that each one had come here to see Doctor DeMarr, for who was better at treating a hypochondriac than a quack?

'I've developed a polyp,' Mr Henry Byron Haggin told Gerald, the old man tapping himself on the lower buttons of his shirtfront.

The president of the United States had a polyp. It was on the television news. Gerald had seen it – seen the polyp, too – on the Cape, at the cottage.

'Do you have any substantial reason for thinking this, Mr Haggin?'

'A swelling and a pronounced tenderness,' Mr Haggin said, seeming to quote, 'in my abdominal area.'

'You're quite a diagnostician.'

Gerald found it easy to smile at the patient from across his businesslike desk.

'Yes. This polyp as I say is in my lower intestine.'

So was the president's polyp.

'Would you mind taking your shirt off, Mr Haggin?'

The large feeble man sighed and obeyed and then sat hunched forward, his big pale belly upright and swollen, like an unwrapped joint of meat he held in his lap – loin of pork, something damp and disgusting until it was cooked.

57

Gerald asked him to sit up straight, and then he felt for the polyp with his fingertips as Mr Haggin winced.

'We'll have to have you in for tests,' Gerald said.

Mr Haggin smiled; that was how the president's polyp had been dealt with.

When there were no more patients, Gerald could think clearly – and it was then that he realized that he had not consciously tried to imitate George. He had not been aware of impersonating his brother. He had been himself, without any pretence. It was his own triumph – George had had no part in it. Gerald's skill was his common sense. It was not necessary to think about George. But when he reflected on his success he decided that it had not arisen out of imitation but was instead a result of his having improved upon George. He was, simply, better than his brother: 'There's something different... You're happy.'

The day had started with a burial; but that burial had set him free.

He could not show his delight. He didn't dare. And yet his feeling of satisfaction relaxed him and made him solemnly garrulous – he wanted to take that woman Tallis into his confidence.

'I think I should tell you the reason for my shock,' he said. She had come into his office with the same suffering look that had touched his heart when he had first seen her. He realized that she was the first young person he had ever wanted to help.

She said, 'It's not necessary –'

'Please, stay.'

She turned to him, looking apprehensive. 'If it'll make you feel better.'

'It was my brother. He died over the weekend.'

He was then very sorry he had said it. Tallis looked stunned, and Gerald imagined for a moment that she had stopped breathing. He saw how thin she was – so frail in her summer clothes – and he saw, too, a stiffness, a teetering resignation. Tallis looked like someone who had just drowned.

'Are you all right?' he said. He found himself reassuring her.

She said in a slow, underwater voice, 'I didn't even know you had a brother.'

5

He had taken possession of the office; now he unlocked the door of George's apartment on the next floor and sized it up. It was empty and cool on this summer evening, and its stillness said that it had been abandoned. It was hard to be in a dead man's home and not think that you were in a tomb: it brought back his old buried-alive feeling.

The place was very orderly, and moving from room to room Gerald saw that George had lived here alone. It was obvious in the undisturbed order of the rooms, the walled-in shadows, the position of the one large chair, the single taste in the décor – orangey walls, an unlikely terracotta colour that was, Gerald thought, perfect really. The bathroom – everything in it – told him that only one person used it, a vain and rather foolish man who pampered himself in a superficial and self-deceiving way and lingered here in that silk bathrobe, among these mirrors and these expensive bottles, looking at his own awful face.

George was dead. Gerald searched the rooms for drugs. Perhaps there were none here; perhaps they were well hidden. In any case, it was a mistake he had no intention of making – it had killed George, so it would save him: George's death gave him life.

Apart from the drugs, George's life had been fairly tidy. Gerald saw that he could make it perfect.

He found the liquor cabinet and poured himself a glass of vodka. He threw open the windows for the evening breeze. He was high enough so that the street noise was muffled, even somewhat comforting – a low clatter and drone, adding to the raffish atmosphere of this downtown apartment. The bedroom had a textile smell – curtains and bedspread, and what were those ridiculous candles doing on the dresser? But when Gerald lit them he saw the room in a new way, the flames jumping on the wall, the mirrors on the headboard of the bed glittering, and he savoured the sweet tang of warm wax. He filled his glass again and tried to resist gulping it. But his thirst was powerful – all those years of dullness and denial, his shadow life as a twin. He drank and soon he possessed the apartment too.

Before he was fully drunk he took a shower, believing it would sober him. He changed into one of George's lightweight suits. What pleasure it gave him to pull on those socks and slip on the jacket – a perfect fit. The low chair was just the right height.

He thought: It had to be George, because he was small enough to fit into the barrel.

He instantly forgot that thought.

What am I trying to remember?

Something – a crystal – began to form from broken splinters in his mind. He took another drink to help it along, and then he sensed it dissolve. He was glad it was gone. He suspected that it had been a fear.

The phone rang. He was laughing softly as he answered.

It was Tallis. Already this life seemed wholly circumscribed!

'I hope you don't think I was being insensitive. I am very sorry about your brother. If I had known he existed I think I might have been able to say something sensible. But it was such a surprise – that you had a brother, that he was dead.'

Gerald said, 'Why not come over?'

His triumphant feeling, which was a feeling of wonderful lungs, had returned to him with her call.

'Would it help?' She was presumably thinking of the death. In a guarded way she said, 'I'm still a little afraid of you. And it's late.'

He was glad she said that, because he was a little afraid of her. But she had spoken first: he felt protected by her fear.

He said, 'The way you touched me today –'

There was a sound of air in the phone – had she sighed?

He said, 'I felt like someone completely different. I was alive, in a kind of time warp. Nothing else mattered. I wanted you so much. You'll never know how that reassured me. Energy passed through your hand and strengthened me, and –'

He faltered, becoming self-conscious at her prolonged silence and wondering how long he had been talking – was it minutes or hours? He felt enlarged and noisy and stupid with vodka. He was afraid in a helpless way that he had gone too far with her and had been talking through his hat.

Still she said nothing.

'Are you there?'

He forgot her name.

'Yes,' she said. 'It's strange hearing you say that.' Had he blundered?

'That was one of the first things you ever said to me.'

What had he said?

'You're so sweet, George,' she said sorrowfully.

This was perfection. What was it the woman patient had said? *You always say that.* Perfection.

Tallis said, 'You have changed, haven't you?'

'Yes, yes,' he said. 'What is it?'

She was crying now, and in trying to stifle the sobs she was making them more distinct.

'You know what I need,' she said at last.

But her sobs had frightened him. He said, 'Maybe you're right. It is pretty late.'

'You've got a terrible day tomorrow,' she said.

Another mystery. He said, 'Excuse me?' pretending he hadn't heard it, so that she would rephrase it – perhaps explain it.

'Those scary-looking guys are coming tomorrow,' she said.
That didn't help.

'But I'm pretty desperate, too. What about tomorrow night? If
you really mean it.'

'I mean it!'

In saying so he convinced himself that he had known her for
years and understood her. And as if to prove it, in that same
moment he remembered her name.

'I mean it, Tallis.'

'We'll do it the old way and take our time, like we used to.'

'Yes,' he said, 'like we used to,' and saw it all – candles, mirrors,
her long pale body in his bed, and her shadow making a witch on
the wall.

He was asleep soon after that, and all night the roaring in his
ears from the traffic in Kenmore Square had a sound like a
slipstream and gave him dreams.

Just before he woke he dreamed of a woman whom he was
passing on Boylston Street. 'What are you doing here?' she
mouthed. She was small and old, she had a child's face. She drew
a gun from out of her oversize coat and shot Gerald in the chest.
He sank slowly, sinking to his knees with each step. It was a toy
pistol – he had known that before it went off – and yet the
woman's face had terrified him. The woman was his mother.

While he was dressing the dream came to him – the pistol first,
then the rest of it. But what fascinated him was the realization
that he had had that same dream ten thousand times or more. He
just now grasped that he had been dreaming it most nights of his
life.

A patient was waiting in the reception area. This was the reason
Tallis greeted Gerald in a formal way.

'Good morning, Doctor.'

Gerald smiled, thinking: Doctor of what?

63

But he was pleased. There was something about Tallis's formality that suggested there was passion beneath it – exactly like the fine grey suit she had on: it was for him. She was being efficient, giving nothing away; it distracted and aroused him.

She has made love to me before, he thought. Soon, I'll make love to her.

'Any messages?' he said. When she handed over the sheaf of pink slips he muttered, 'Prescriptions, prescriptions.'

She said, 'Are you surprised?'

'I couldn't find my prescription pad yesterday,' he said.

'On your desk.'

'No' – he had looked for it, he was absolutely sure.

Today the pad lay at the corner of the blotter. Gerald thought: I must be careful.

The patient was Murray U. Stone. Gerald saw from his file that he was eighty-six years old. He was full of complaints – back pains, indigestion, sleeplessness, wind. How strange that this man on the verge of death should care about his stomach and his sleep – he was snatching at another month of life. The old man thought it might be his prostate – that was the sort of thing he had to expect at his time of life, wasn't it?

Gerald quizzed him on his diet and told him to cut down on ice cream.

Mr Stone wanted to go on living. Two days earlier, Gerald would have found this pointless and selfish, and in an old man a kind of insanity. Now he saw the point of it. He sympathized with the trembling man. It wasn't such a crazy wish, and Gerald was all the more attentive when he remembered the humiliation and boredom of his own other life.

'Aren't you going to have a poke at my prostate?' the old man said.

64   In time, Gerald thought, I will understand this business. But it

was not a job – it was a whole life. Already he had begun to accept its demands. He was glad of that: he wanted to live this life. But there were certain tasks he could not perform. He could not carry out a convincing examination, he was too disgusted by the sight of their underwear to be able to concentrate; he couldn't write prescriptions, he knew nothing of drugs.

He was made speechless, or at least short of breath, by their nakedness. Poor pale flesh – it did not fit them. So he stalled. He played charades with the stethoscope, he muttered. He sent Mr Stone away with a tube of ointment he had found in a box of samples.

Mr Libby, the next patient, entered the office bent double, as if he was straining to touch his toes. He stayed in this stooped position, speaking sideways about wanting to see a chiropractor.

Gerald was genuinely annoyed that Mr Libby wanted to be recommended to a specialist. He said, 'Don't you trust me to treat you?' and fished out a bottle of Valium from among the samples.

'Valium's for depression,' Mr Libby said.

'It has many uses,' Gerald said in a peevish way. It was the one drug he understood and this stupid man was contradicting him! 'It relaxes muscles – all muscles. That's why it's good for tension, that's why it's good for bad backs. Don't you want to get better?'

There were phone calls after that – demands for prescriptions. They made him feel inadequate. He considered taking a vacation – maybe to Florida, where he could bribe a pharmacist to show him how to write prescriptions for the important drugs. With a professional letterhead on his pad and a medical degree on the wall, he could make it all look legitimate. It was not dishonest, he felt – it was just complicated and hard to explain. But it was idealism all the same. He saw it clearly, and then it struck him that it was exactly what George had done.

I'll find another way, he thought.

That was the morning. He was wondering whether to go out for lunch when Tallis buzzed him and said in a whisper, 'Mr Scarfo's just got out of the elevator.'

He heard the thump of the reception room door and, almost in the same moment, his own door was shoved open and the man was upon him, with Tallis close behind, handing Gerald the man's file.

Mr Scarfo was young and haggard. He had a grey complexion and yellowish eyes, and he limped – but he seemed careless rather than crippled. He was thin and round-shouldered, like an awkward boy. His hair was tangled, he needed a shave. He wore a wrinkled shirt, and it was from the pocket of this that he took a folded-over swatch of twenty-dollar bills. He placed the money on the desk.

'I'm not going to argue with you this time,' Mr Scarfo said. 'Just give me the prescription and I'll go.'

'You'll have to be a bit more specific,' Gerald said.

'You know what I'm talking about.'

The gaps between his teeth seemed to indicate that he was unintelligent. Yet the man was persistent and oddly energetic – dry-mouthed in a nervous sort of way, but defiant, like all the other hypochondriacs he had seen in this office. But which others had tried to palm money to him?

'I've been having a hard time,' Mr Scarfo said.

Gerald had concealed the file, but even so there was nothing on it when he quietly sneaked a look – the name and address, nothing else; no record of illness, no prescriptions.

Mr Scarfo was still talking: 'And these doctors you re-commended – they wouldn't give me anything.'

'I'm sorry about that,' Gerald said, trying to calm the man with a show of sympathy.

'And you went away,' Mr Scarfo said. 'I was sick. I didn't know what to do.'

'Let's have a look at you,' Gerald said, and reached for his stethoscope.

This made Mr Scarfo angry. 'You're always doing that. You're stalling. You're wasting my time. Are you going to give me a prescription or not?'

Gerald said in a kindly way, 'I can't give you anything at the moment.'

'I told you the last time, I'm running out of stuff. I won't have any in a few days – and then what?' But he did not wait for a reply. He said, 'It's not fair!'

Gerald said, 'I want to help –'

'You *have* to help,' Mr Scarfo said. 'You gave prescriptions to three people I know, four hundred bucks apiece. This is five hundred, Doctor –'

'I don't want your money.'

'Rizzo – you gave him one. I seen it!' Mr Scarfo stood up, and even though Gerald himself was standing the man towered over him. 'I could pinch your head off so easy.'

For the first time, Gerald became frightened. He did not know anything about narcotics. He could humour a patient, but this was something different: he was helpless.

'And a guy named Ferrara. You gave him one!'

Who were these people and what had he given them?

Gerald moved away from Mr Scarfo, to place a safe distance between them. He did not want to argue. He wanted the money, he wanted this life, and he already hated this man enough to give him exactly what he wanted, and the more lethal the better. But he resisted. This was precisely where George had gone wrong.

'You'll have to go,' Gerald said.

'I'm not moving.'

'I'll call the police.'

'Beautiful,' Mr Scarfo said. 'Then I'll tell the police about all the shit you got for these other guys.'

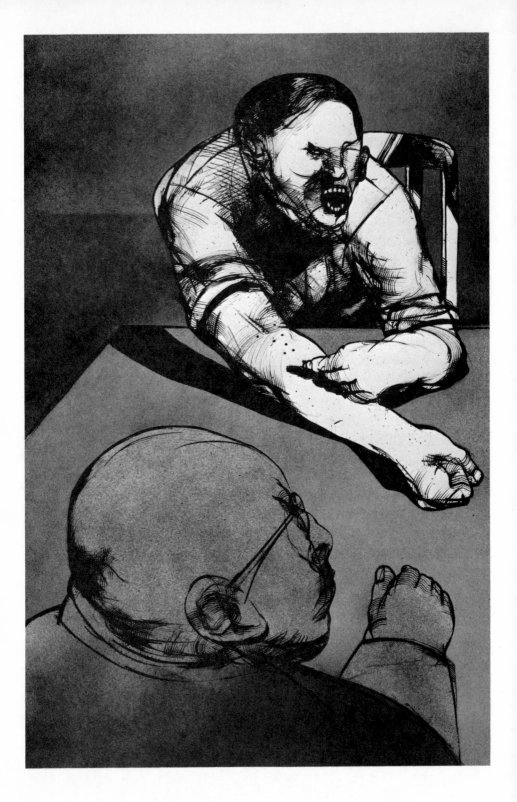

'If you do,' Gerald said crisply, inspired by his anger, 'I'll never get anything for you. Are you willing to risk that?'

Mr Scarfo stood up. He said, 'I'll be back.'

It was a snarl, a threat – he spoke it darkly; and it rattled Gerald terribly. It was now after two o'clock, with another patient on the way. There was no time for lunch.

The next patient had a similar request to Mr Scarfo's. This was Toby – another blank file: he was underweight, twenty or so, with a skeletal smile: clearly ill and addicted. He said, 'How about it?'

'I can't help you,' Gerald said.

'That's what you said the last time.'

Good, Gerald thought. He said, 'I want you to understand that.'

'I don't understand nothing. You cost me a lot of money. I paid for this office. That desk. That crappy lamp. That's my money.'

Gerald resented the young man's tone, and the mention of the lamp – he particularly liked the stainless steel desk lamp. There was much in the office that he realized he had wanted his whole life.

'I can't give you a prescription,' he said.

'I think you like saying that. It gives you a sense of power. You're paranoid.'

Gerald hated ignorant people who used technical or pompous words to intimidate him. The young man was stupid, and yet Gerald was hurt by his insolence. He suspected that it did not arise from the young man's own weakness but rather from his seeing that Gerald was helpless.

'Your time is up,' Gerald said, feeling trapped.

'I'm leaving, but I'm not going anywhere. Get it?' He stood up. 'I'll be around.'

There was another phone call: 'You were recommended.' There was a man named Hume who said the pimple on the back of his neck was a boil that needed lancing. And there was Archdale.

69

Archdale was a Harvard student; he looked pathetic with his thick grubby textbooks, and Gerald knew before the boy spoke that he wanted a prescription. Archdale pleaded. He had money with him, he said. He looked worried and began to cry, saying that he might be able to get more.

'Please,' Gerald said. He wondered whether he should offer to examine him. He was afraid to touch him.

He said, 'You've been here before, haven't you?'

'Yes –'

And then Gerald saw that it was in this that George had gone wrong. He thought: I will not become George.

Archdale had not heard him. He was still talking, saying, 'I realized what it was. You didn't want money any more. You said no –'

Had George said no?

'It's very smart, really. It's a kind of strength, saying you don't want money any more.'

Gerald did not know what to say.

'I can't buy you, because you've already got money,' Archdale said. 'But ask yourself – how did you make all that money?'

Now the young man was going, but he paused at the door.

'Ask yourself.'

When the young man was gone, Gerald was so shaken he told Tallis that he could not see any more patients. He had begun to understand how messy George's life had been: he did not want to make the same mistakes. He needed time, in order to succeed.

He said, 'I'm going up to my apartment.'

'What time do you want us to meet?'

He had forgotten that – anxiety had taken away his desire. He wanted to be alone, but he did not have the heart to tell her. What would George have done?

He said, as candidly as he could, 'I'm not sure about tonight.'

'What do you mean by that?'

He was vague because he was tired and fearful, but she seemed to think it was lack of interest.

Before he could reply, Tallis said coldly, 'I never know whether to trust you.'

'You can trust me,' he said, trying hard to reassure her.

She smiled. She said, 'You let me down once.' Her smile broke and she began to cry. The weeping had a ruinous effect on her. She looked like one of the most unhealthy people he had ever seen, and a great deal sicker than any of his patients.

He felt pity for her. No other person so young had ever moved him in that way.

6

Pitying her, Gerald felt powerful and kindly. Her weakness roused him. He was happy and hopeful, because he knew that he could help her. Unlike George, he could be good to her. Certainly George had born some responsibility for her. *You let me down once* – that was a judgement on George.

Gerald drew courage from his knowledge that he only resembled his brother in a physical way. Inwardly he was another man entirely. His private image was of two identical bottles, the same shape and size and colour; but one contained poison and the other its antidote. And that was also why only one person in the world could heal this woman; only one woman deserved his love.

He said, 'Tallis' and touched her, and she looked at him with such passion that he wanted to hold her and kiss her. And as always, when he looked hard at her, she seemed desperately afraid and forlorn.

The Maison Rouge on Newbury Street was a restaurant that Gerald often fantasized about being in, with a woman, drinking wine by candlelight.

'You and your French restaurants,' Tallis said, but warily as though she was afraid of going too far. Had she been there before with George? Would the waiter remember? Would the waiter remember George's credit card and see that Gerald's was not the same? Of course not.

She was wearing a long-sleeved dress, silky black, with a pattern shimmering on the fabric. The pallor of her skin that had made her seem so ill now gave her a haunting beauty. Her face was thin and intense, and she did not take her eyes from his.

She said, 'I can hardly believe this.'

Gerald, enjoying himself and happier than he could remember, took her fragile hand and held it gently.

'You look lovely,' he said and, inhaling her perfume, he could not stop himself from saying, 'Lavender. It's so familiar –'

'Your mother used to wear this perfume,' Tallis said.

It was true – she knew everything except who he was. But what mattered was that she and George had a long past, a history that included secrets and intimacies and perhaps passion – almost certainly passion. Gerald was shocked by how much she knew, but he was emboldened by the one crucial fact she did not know. Her ignorance gave him power. But he did not want power – he wanted love, friendship, the sort of happiness he felt at this moment.

He said, 'Why shouldn't we always be as happy as this?'

'You know why,' Tallis said. She was suddenly resentful. 'You've made it so hard for me. You've put me through hell.'

He stared at her. He had to be mute. He was the ignorant one now.

'I almost didn't come tonight,' Tallis said and lowered her eyes.

'Look at me,' he said, at once inspired, and when she refused to obey he said it again, urging her, 'Tallis – look at me.'

She was ashamed, he guessed that, and she was angry. She was slight but her will-power gave her an aura of largeness, as though she were bulkily built. And there was a suggestion of violence and danger in her silence.

So was it to be one of those dinners, where the woman agreed to join him for a meal only to use the occasion to scream at him or weep and tell him how he had failed her? One of those testing dinners, like a set of hurdles, where the woman made him submit to her abuse before she rewarded him much later – always too late – with sex, and not enough of that. Please no, he thought.

She was crying again. He had forgotten that he still held her hand in his. He released it – his own hand was no larger. Her small size would certainly have made her attractive to George. There was so much that Gerald would have asked her about him.

Tallis said something tear-sodden and inaudible. Gerald asked her softly to repeat it.

'I feel terrible,' she said.

It was an unhelpful and ambiguous statement, yet he was overcome by his feeling for her, and he began to babble.

He said, 'Please don't worry, my darling. Let me pour you a drink. This is how I want it to be from now on. Let me feed you, let me love you –'

He poured the wine. He caught sight of the label. He said, 'This Schramsberg *blanc de blanc* is as good as any French champagne you can name. Thirty-eight dollars is nothing. The Krug is over a hundred. California wine is vastly underrated by wine snobs. They pay no attention to the vintage Mondavis. Your Sonomas. Your Niebaum-Coppolas.'

Now she smiled and her mood lifted.

'Oh, George,' she said, and sighed. 'Why do you always pretend to know about wine? You know it's all booze to you, just another anaesthetic.'

'You like it, at any rate.'

She looked piercingly at him.

'You know what I like,' she said.

Gerald could not go on looking into those eyes. He glanced down, but her voice found him and pierced him further. 'You know what I want,' she said.

What was it? Her hand reached his leg, her fingers gripped him.

'You know what I need.'

Only when the waiter approached them again did she let go. And then she said she wasn't hungry. She said she would have some pheasant consommé and a small salad. Gerald ordered the lobster bisque to start, and he told the waiter he was torn between the *goujons* of monkfish and the tuna *niçoise*. The waiter pursed his lips as though in warning that he had a thick French accent, and he said that it was yellowfin tuna, from Hawaii, and it was fresh – and something in the way he lisped, making a fishmouth on the word fresh, made Gerald choose the *goujons*.

Tallis' expression still said *You know what I need.*

He felt he did know. He loved being in the presence of this woman, and as though for the first time ever he saw the point of eating a meal with someone you desire – being near to her, so close to her face as she ate gracefully, putting food into her mouth and smiling and returning his gaze, watching him. This sort of tempting meal was a way of controlling and exciting desire. He wanted it to continue, he wanted to go on looking at her, stroking her with his eyes.

In the past such meals had been painful for him. He had sat like a man being judged. The woman across from him forked food into her turned-down mouth and wore a sour expression, as though she were about to choke. Yet she would go on chewing and frowning, looking disgusted, as though the whole experience happened to be physically painful. *Take the prisoner away.*

He was sorry that this woman Tallis had shared a past with George – sorry for her, for what she had had to endure. But that same awkward past helped him too. The preliminaries were over, and that was always the embarrassing part: Gerald had always been too slow or too fast. Only his letters had ever really worked, but they were letters to strangers. George had begun with Tallis, but Gerald could carry on from there – loving her, pleasing her, impressing her. He had a strong assurance, as he sat there eating in the Maison Rouge, that he was already her lover. That suspicion made him very calm, and it steadied him in his chair.

'I haven't told you anything about my week off,' Gerald said. 'Don't you want to hear the details?'

Tallis looked alarmed – the same look of anxious surprise which had been on her face when he'd stepped out of the elevator that first time.

She said, 'Why do you always smile like that when you're angry?'

'I'm not angry.'

'When you're accusing me of something,' she said.

'I'm not accusing you.'

'I don't want to hear the details of your week off,' she said.

He reached for her hand once more, and he said, 'I don't think I've ever told you about the time I was in Vietnam.'

'That's practically all you ever talk about,' she said. 'But I don't want to hear about how you almost became an addict. I don't want to hear drug stories. Talking about dope makes me want a fix.'

Her talking reassured him. So George fantasized too – or had George really served there?

He told his snake story. He said, 'We were out on patrol one day and got pinned down by the Cong. Under fire for about six-seven hours – and I was lying there, firing back, lobbing grenades, waiting for air-cover. Suddenly the firing stopped and we decided to move on. As I walked along I started to limp. I looked down and saw that a huge snake was coiled around my ankle.'

Gerald smiled at her; she smiled back. She didn't look the least bit impressed.

'God, you've got a terrible memory,' she said.

'What do you mean?' He hated saying it.

'*Then* what happened? You always tell me about the snake, but you never tell me how you got it off your ankle!'

Gerald leaned forward, as though to kiss her. 'That's the point,' he said. 'Let's go, I want to tell you later.'

In the car he remembered that it was his father's story – a Cape story: his father sitting on a grassy bank and the copperhead coiling itself on his ankle. The old man had never revealed how he had rid himself of the thing. Perhaps he too had been lying.

Tallis said, 'Where are you taking me?'

'Guess.'

She was eager, and in the elevator, when they kissed – his first with her, but that kiss had a turbulent history, he knew – she hugged him tightly, seeming to cling fearfully, until she opened her eyes and looked at him.

He wanted nothing to change. He held her and hoped. And in the apartment – George's apartment, but already Gerald felt at home and confident enough to walk through it in the dark – he did not switch on the light. He sat with Tallis on the sofa, loving the delay, savouring his fantasies.

'You know what I want.'

'I want you too.'

Wasn't that what she meant? She seemed to be frowning in the dark. He kissed her and found that her face was wet with tears. Had she always wept this way with George?

'I thought you never wanted to see me again,' she said.

'No,' he said, in a moan of protest.

'I thought you hated me.'

Gerald held her tightly, though he was aware of her fragile bones, the basket of them beneath her silky dress.

'I thought I hated you,' she said, and she shuddered. 'It was a nightmare.'

Gerald was fumbling with the dress, pushing at it. Tallis lay back on the cushions, and he felt her body with his fingers as he murmured over her, swallowing, breathing hard, blinded by his own eagerness.

He was abruptly shoved back, as she stiffened and protected herself with her thin arms, to keep him away. She cried out but it was not a human noise – it was a cat's hiss.

'What's wrong?' Gerald said, in a fearful voice.

'Who are you?' Tallis said, and edged away from him and switched on the light.

Gerald stood up and dragged at his trousers as he staggered. It was a clumsy gesture of surrender. He was on the point of telling her everything.

'Oh, George, I'm so sorry.'

And she knelt before him and held him.

'You seemed like a stranger in the dark,' she said.

After that, they made love. The darkness that made her timid turned him into a little brute and at one moment he thought he might have hurt her badly. But he realized when she shrugged it off that he was small and harmless and that she was, even in her weakness, much stronger than he would ever be.

She woke him once in the night, moaning, 'Help me, George,' and he pretended not to hear. Later when the early sunshine of summer knifed the blinds she said, 'You will help me, won't you?'

He said he would, he wanted to more than anything else.

He kissed her. If he had seemed to her like a stranger in the darkness, she seemed in this embrace like the most desperate creature he had ever touched, and he promised again to help her.

'It would make everything right,' she said.

That was exactly how he felt.

Help – that was all she wanted. He was glad that she had asked. Was there any better way for him to prove his love to her? He felt that he owed her his life, for she had already helped him, by rousing his desire. He was forty-six years old. Two years before, a woman had left him. He had not regretted her departure. She was the one who had sent his letters back – those wonderful witty letters. He had thought: How could I ever have pleased her? His sexual charge was diminished, flickering out – soon, he had felt, he would not need a woman, and then he would be truly alone.

But Tallis had changed that. From the moment he had seen her he had desired her, and he had been thrilled by a renewed hope in the future. He became optimistic, he felt younger, he wanted this woman.

Because his desire for her was new to him and revealed new aspects of himself – that was why. It gave him hope. Love was another word for life – real life, real vitality. Loving Tallis he could live longer and be happier. He wanted to go on being that loving man, and for that to happen he needed this woman as his lover.

She left early to go home and change, but she was back in the office before nine, her sallow complexion and her thin face still giving her an odd vulnerable beauty, that of a frail child.

There was a patient at nine-fifteen; Tallis showed the girl in. She was very formal now – 'Here is Miss Franda's file, Doctor.' 'Thank you, Miss Jordan.' The charade thrilled Gerald, because under all the formality desire lay like an ache, and he clearly saw their struggling sexuality of just a few hours ago. That secret was an excitement. And it was surely something that the brusque George had never known.

When the patient, Gail Franda – she was just eighteen – seated herself in the examining room, Gerald went to the lobby and smiled at Tallis. He went near to her and touched her face. He said, 'I love you.'

She looked pleadingly at him. Her eyes were grey flecked with green.

Miss Franda's file listed a two-year history of bulimia, a condition Gerald was familiar with – Dot Vincenzo at the Navy Yard office (first at the cash desk, then in Receipts) had a daughter (Lauren? Lorraine? Lorretta?), a model, who binged and purged. Why was it that the word model always seemed like a synonym for prostitute? And yet models apparently worked very hard. Bulimia was not sexual, not at all, Dot had explained – not like

79

anorexia, which was very suspect. Bulimia had to do with self-image, a girl's shape – her figure, how she thought she ought to look, usually too thin. And yet she would gorge and wolf everything in sight before sticking her finger down her throat.

Surprisingly, Miss Franda was plump.

She said, 'I've started again. Last weekend, at my cousin's wedding. I ate like a horse. I was up the whole night.'

'The main thing to remember is that bulimia is not sexual in origin,' Gerald said.

'That's what you always say, Doctor –'

George had told her *that?*

Miss Franda was still talking '– but eating is sort of sexual, isn't it?'

'Of course it depends on what you eat,' Gerald said, wondering whether he was stalling or making a valid point.

But the problem – the reason for Miss Franda's visit today – was that she didn't know whether to tell her mother. She wasn't asking for medication. She simply wanted to know if she should tell the woman that it had begun again and that she was determined to work on it.

Gerald urged her to confide in her mother and then to return when she had her mother's reaction.

'We can work on it together,' Gerald said, and thought: I would have made a good psychiatrist.

Mrs Caputo's son just had a sore throat, but typically she claimed it was tonsillitis. That was the hypochondriac's characteristic response to an ailment: making it much worse, turning every lump into a tumour, preferably malignant.

Gerald told the silent feverish boy to open up, and using a wooden tongue depresser he looked into the quivering mouth.

'It's a sore throat,' Gerald said. 'I'd advise plenty of rest and liquids.'

'He's in agony, he can't swallow,' Mrs Caputo said. 'Why don't you put him on a course of antibiotics.'

They imagined their ailments! They imagined their cures!

Gerald smiled tolerantly and made sure Mrs Caputo registered the smile. He said, 'Do you want a violent case of diarrhoea on your hands? Do you want a child in full spate? Because that's what penicillin usually means to an eight-year-old.'

'What about tetracyclin?' Mrs Caputo said, looking obstinate.

Gerald chuckled at the woman. 'I'll do the prescribing around here, Mrs Caputo, if that's okay.'

He did not say, though the knowledge stung him, that he was unable to write a prescription for an antibiotic or any other drug. But so what? People were better off without them. He was not going to encourage them in their hypochondria, as George obviously had.

Yet they weren't all hypochondriacs. He had more phone calls – two sounding distinctly threatening, demanding prescriptions, saying they would stop by. Another man was almost in tears – desperate, he said. And the last was from Scarfo.

Scarfo said, 'I'm coming over. You better have something for me.'

That thuggish voice. Wasn't there any way he could be stopped? And yet Gerald wished he knew what Scarfo knew, because Scarfo knew George.

The only afternoon patient was a man with a loose thumbnail and an infection at its base. It was a deranged and ugly thing his file called a paronychia. Gerald looked it up in George's well-thumbed medical dictionary (it shared a shelf with an equally well-thumbed *Physicians' Desk Reference*). Then he looked again at the swollen thumb and curling nail.

'It seems to be healing nicely,' Gerald said. And he scissored off the rest of the bandage and dressed it again, using a method he had learned in Boy Scouts, First Aid merit badge.

Scarfo appeared as the man with the paronychia was leaving. He ignored Tallis. He loomed at Gerald's door and without hesitating entered, slamming the door shut. He was big and unshaven.

'I can't help you.'

'I want a fix right now,' Scarfo said. 'Then I need a prescription for more. You're going to give it to me.'

Gerald said, 'If you don't leave my office this minute, I'm going to call the police.' He picked up the phone. He stabbed at the numbers. 'You think I'm kidding?'

It worked, and Gerald was amazed at how quickly it did.

Scarfo backed away, but before he left he said, 'There's lots of other suppliers, I'll get some. But you've been jerking me around – lying to me. I know you're a dealer. I'll be back. Think about it. You're going to pay for those lies.'

And Gerald thought: George was hiding from Scarfo – obviously. But why, if George was an addict and a dealer – the classic conundrum, the sick doctor – had he stopped supplying drugs to these people?

Tallis was also asking for drugs. That was the help she wanted. She entered as soon as Scarfo had left. She said, 'I've locked the office.'

Gerald's desire was roused by her simple statement and an awareness of their isolation here.

Tallis was pulling the blinds shut as Gerald held her and kissed her.

'First I need a fix,' she said.

'After,' he said, and drew her closer to him.

With that promise and hope brightening her eyes, Tallis responded to him, and then slipped her dress off and lay on the sofa.

'Take the rest of my clothes off,' she said.

Gerald approached her with trembling hands.

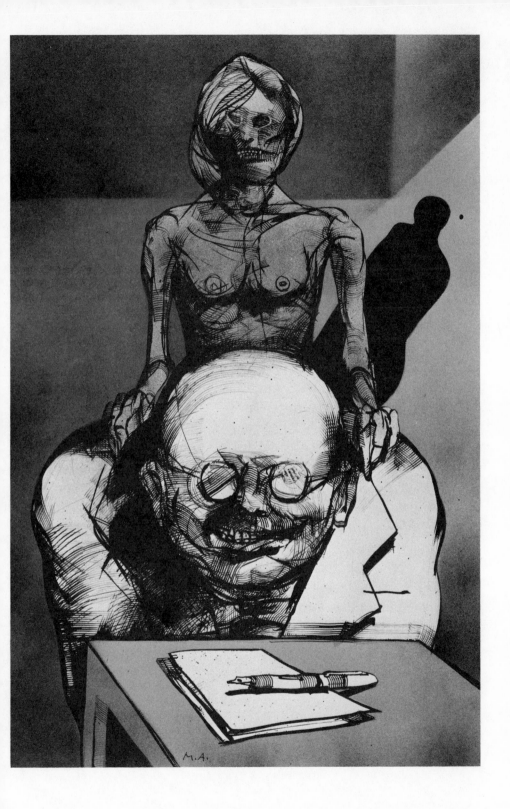

'Now, George, now,' Tallis said, and woke him – he had fallen into a doze from the effort of making love to her. He got to his feet and dressed and kissed her tenderly.

'I'll be right back.'

But he was desperate. He knew he couldn't write a prescription. He wondered what drugs he could find in the city.

He took a taxi to the lower end of Tremont, where it began to decay, and he walked, lurking, seeking a likely person. He saw a black man and held his gaze. The man offered marijuana. Gerald said he needed heroin.

'I don't deal that shit,' the man said, and seemed offended. 'That stuff's death. It fuck you up.'

Then it was dark, and he was too frightened to walk farther. He went back to the office and found Tallis crouched on a chair, breathing hard, shivering, clearly suffering.

Gerald took her cold fingers and said, 'I will help you. But it may take a while.'

Tallis said with sudden bitterness, 'I thought you'd changed.'

'I have changed,' Gerald said, trusting the truth of it. He was a different man! 'I'll prove it. I love you.'

'I hate you for saying that.'

'Give me until tomorrow.'

'I can't wait until tomorrow,' Tallis said. 'You're incredible. This is exactly what happened the last time. You bastard.' She watched him hurry to the door. She said, 'You're going again.'

'It's very important.'

She didn't blink. She said coldly, 'That's what you said the last time.'

7

Scarfo's home was in East Boston – according to the file – a sharp right turn after the tunnel, all tenements and hanging laundry, and big badly-made houses intersected by narrow streets. He had left the taxi at the first set of traffic lights, and now he was walking. He walked down London Street, past Lombardo's Lounge, into the maze of three-decker houses. From the airport came the roar and boom of planes, but here the night-time noises were clear voices, dishes being clanked in a sink, television laughter in little bursts of pressure, and the whispers of people in the darkness of their porches and front steps and wooden fire escapes. The sounds were unselfconscious and strangely intimate. The neighbourhood was poor Italian; it smelled of laundry and cooking – scorched tomatoes especially. Roy's Cold Cuts, Gino's Autobody, Christie's Pizza, Homemade Slush, a café or a meatmarket on every corner. The dark cluttered air gave Gerald the sense that he was walking under water.

He turned into Bennington Street and saw the house. The newness of it surprised him: it was in bright repair. In a row of tall square-sided tenements, wood-framed, with dingy scratched shingles on their fronts, this house had white-trimmed windows and fringed awnings, a screened-in piazza and brick steps. It was a proud little bungalow. Gerald was bewildered and somewhat encouraged by it.

He had been frightened. He had gone there wondering what decision to take. If the house had been a decaying tenement he might have been too fearful to knock, he would have gone away. But his curiosity overcame his timidity: the house did not tally with the man. He had not decided what to say, but now at least he could discuss matters. He wanted to help; he did not want to make George's mistakes. Scarfo's threat had truly terrified him.

Walking past, he saw movement inside – people behind curtains, a woman in a kitchen window, and in another room a flickering blue phosphorescence on the ceiling from a television screen.

He could make a deal – just a simple deal. He would offer to sell him some prescription blanks – or give them to him, providing he used them in another city, providing he would say he had stolen them if he were arrested, providing there were no more threats. It was a compromise, but it made sense and Gerald felt it might rid him of the man.

Gerald was relieved that he could not push drugs on to the young man, because he disliked him enough to do it; he was tempted. Yet he did not have to worry about the morality of it, nor the fact that it was crooked. He simply did not have the skill to write prescriptions.

He rang the bell. He heard, 'I'll get it!'

A small boy came to the door. His T-shirt said RED SOX.

'I want to speak to Mr Scarfo,' Gerald said through the mesh in the screen door.

'Mom!' the boy yelled, turning his back on Gerald.

Standing on the front steps in the darkness, Gerald could see into the house, past the entryway to the foyer and a long corridor. The man did not appear. The child ran to the far end of the corridor, and yelled again.

Gerald saw a young woman in a print dress take off an apron and walk towards him. She seemed happy and unconcerned, and that fascinated him. There was something very private and self-contained in her posture. This was Scarfo's wife? She smiled at Gerald. She said, 'My husband's at work.'

'Sorry to bother you this late,' Gerald said. 'It's just that I was hoping for his signature on our petition' – he took out his chequebook and waved it, certain that the woman could not see it in the dark. 'Do you know about the proposal to raise the tunnel toll to a dollar? It's going to affect all of us – everyone in East Boston.'

'What did you say your name was?'

'Charles Leggate. With an 'e'. I live over on London Street, across from Lombardo's.'

'About the toll, huh?'

'Yes,' Gerald said. 'I don't know about you but I'm furious.'

'The thing is, I don't think Sal wants to be disturbed at the station.'

Station?

Gerald said, 'Right. I won't bother him. I didn't realize he was working nights. The North End's a madhouse. That's where he is, isn't it?'

The woman smiled and said, 'Storrow Drive. That's worse. It's all traffic duty and drug busts.'

'I'll catch him tomorrow. Take care.'

But no sooner had he turned into Visconti than he saw a cab, and hailed it, and told the man to take him to the station house on Storrow Drive. Gerald knew the place – it was just behind the Mass General.

Gerald had to see the man in his uniform, and he wanted the man to see him. That would be enough. He would not be intimidated by this policeman, as George obviously had.

In this new life, in which he had taken over the appearance of George, he wanted everyone to know that he was different. Let them believe that George had changed, he thought. Then I can be myself.

'I'd like to see Officer Scarfo,' Gerald said, to the policeman at the desk.

'Salvie,' the policeman called, turning aside.

Behind him sat Scarfo, just inside a small room, and he was obviously preparing for the evening. He was shining one shoe – the shoe in one hand, the black brush in the other.

He was not the starved wolf of the afternoon, but rather a relaxed policeman – a husband and father – who had been interrupted as he prepared for night duty. He was clean shaven, his hair was combed – he had the rosy just-peeled look of someone who was still damp and pink from his shower. He stood up, slightly unbalanced by the sock on one foot, the uniform shoe on the other. It was Scarfo – transformed.

Seeing him, Gerald stepped back – down the stairs and on to the sidewalk. He decided to run, but just a fraction too late: Scarfo got a glimpse of his face a moment before Gerald dashed off.

'What are you doing here?'

Gerald ran, in a panicky way, frightened by the slap of his feet on the sidewalk. Later, after he was safe in a taxi and speeding through the tunnel, he remembered that the barefoot man could never have caught him. He had another recollection – that it had all happened before: he had experienced that whole episode – discovery and chase – from an old dream.

He went to George's apartment on Kenmore Square, but only to get rid of his brother's unlucky clothes and to find a telephone number. Tallis's. She would be back in her own place by now.

'It's me,' he said. He did not want to say George. That was over.

Tallis said, 'What's wrong? Where have you been? Why do you sound so –'

'I've just found Scarfo,' he said. Tallis said nothing. He said, 'Did you hear me?'

'I heard you.' Her voice had gone cold.

'Tallis – he's a phoney. He's completely different. He's a cop!' He was struggling against her silence.

'Are you listening?'

Tallis said, 'Where have you really been?'

'I'm trying to tell you. Scarfo's house. I saw him at home!'

'You got to be lying.'

'He was trying to set me up!' Gerald said. 'He's no junkie. He wanted to get me arrested.'

She said, 'Do we have to go through all this again?'

'It's serious.'

'Yes, but it's not news. You knew what Scarfo was up to. You're making excuses.'

'I'm scared, Tallis.'

She said, 'Exactly what you said before, when you ran out on me.'

He could not speak.

She said, 'You haven't changed at all. You really have lost your nerve.'

'I have changed,' he said. 'I'm going straight – no more phoney prescriptions, no more lies. I'm going to live right.'

She said, 'I've got to see you. Please don't go away again. You did say we could meet – we're lucky to have another chance, George –'

* * *

George is dead, he thought, I am alive. Being George had given him a taste for life. Before, the thought of dying had not worried him. But now he wanted to live; so he bolted. There was only one place he could go.

He found his old car in the Common Garage. The sense of desperation was still vivid in his mind. George must have felt this way – no, George had felt worse: George was George, and Gerald was himself. George had been fleeing from his only life. Gerald felt some sympathy for his brother now, and when he reached home and locked the door and washed, he looked into the mirror over the sink and saw a resemblance. It must have been something like the face that George had seen in his own mirror. But in Gerald's sympathy there was smugness and relief: he was home, he was safe. He thought: I'm not dead.

And yet he did not sleep well. He had slept much more soundly last night in George's bed. He thrashed, trying to dive and submerge himself in sleep, but each time he ended up on his back, awake, his face to the ceiling, watching car headlights move from one side to the other.

An hour passed; another hour. One set of headlights moved more slowly than the others, then stopped before they reached the far wall. They slid a bar of light across the ceiling, and there it stayed, a slanted stripe over Gerald's bed. He sat up and listened.

The car had entered his driveway. Gerald looked out and saw only shadows inside, though just after turning away from the window he thought he heard the click of a car door being shut very carefully.

Gerald did not bother to dress. He hurried to the back stairs and climbed to the empty apartment on the upper floor where George had been. There he waited, hiding himself, wondering whether to sit down in that dreadful chair. Let them take what they want, he thought, and then he sat down.

He covered his face: My poor brother. He was thinking about himself most of all. He was both of them. And he always felt especially small in the early morning.

Dawn had reached the windows – a yellow-green early morning sky behind the telephone poles, that forest of black crucifixes. There was no sun yet, but instead pale seeping colours that brimmed like liquid around the old house.

The door opened quickly and a large startled man said, 'You're still here.'

Then Gerald was dazzled by the man's flashlight, and the weak sunrise was not strong enough to outshine it. The man was hidden behind it and, perhaps realizing what he had just said, he repeated it in amazement: 'You're still here!'

The light shook as it moved towards Gerald, paralysing and blinding him. He was at the mercy of the man, but the man was breathless – still exclaiming, and almost laughing as he spoke.

'I'm alive,' Gerald said.

'Course you are.'

'Turn off the light – please.'

The man did so. Gerald saw that this large dark man had a short neck – no neck at all really; his head was crammed between his shoulders, and when he turned his head he turned his whole body. But he had the sleepy harmless look of someone who has just woken up. He was still on the verge of laughter, with eager eyes, as if he was listening to a good story and wanting more.

'You know me,' he said. 'Right?'

'No,' Gerald said, and felt safe.

'You don't know me!'

Now the man did laugh, and watching him, Gerald laughed, too. It was a good joke – after all he had been through, he was relieved by the apparition of the laughing man.

Gerald pondered the situation: I think I do know this man. I think I have been here before.

The intimation had been frequent over the past two days: his dreams had prepared him and had made this strangeness familiar. He was sure he had dreamed this: the empty room, the visiting man's unexpected laughter. He had seen it all, more than once.

'Why ain't you asleep?'

That sounded familiar, too!

And when Gerald said, 'I couldn't sleep,' it sounded to him like another echo.

The man's face was bright – he was smiling, perhaps thinking: He should be in bed! There were footsteps on the back stairs. The man wasn't alarmed. He walked easily over to the door and opened it to the visitor, a young woman.

'Tallis,' Gerald said.

Her face was sallow and bony, her clothes were shapeless on her body – they hung in vertical folds. Her thin ankles showed at her trouser cuffs and her little toes were twisted in her sandals.

'He's still here. He says he doesn't know me,' the man said.

Tallis smiled at this – the smile tightened her face and made it even thinner. She approached Gerald with her hands in her pockets.

'It's the same guy!' The large dark man said. 'He woke up!'

Gerald said, 'You're going to laugh when I tell you – you're laughing already – but I really don't . . .'

Only seconds had passed since Tallis had entered the room. But Gerald was fascinated by her. She was all he wanted of George's life. She was lovely in a pitiful way and she looked hungrily at him – still smiling slightly. She had lovely lips and large eyes: they were part of her hunger.

Tallis drew her hand out of her pocket and Gerald saw something between her fingers. She lifted her arm and her sleeve slipped back; and he saw scars and blue punctures where her sleeve had been. She held the pointed thing like a dart. It was so narrow and she was so nimble with it, it seemed like a part of her hand. She found the plunger with her thumb and let the needle glitter at him.

'Now I'll show you how it's done,' Tallis said.

'Are you talking to me?' Gerald said.

'Both of you,' she said.

He thought for a moment that she meant George and him – the idea of George still clung to him, and he had been dragging his brother around like a flat shadow. But no – she meant the man, who was now behind him.

92   'But this time you don't wake up,' Tallis said.